I0687172

Smitten With Death

by

Sharon Saracino

Max Logan Series, Book 3

This is a work of fiction. Names, characters, places, and incidents are either the product of the author's imagination or are used fictitiously, and any resemblance to actual persons living or dead, business establishments, events, or locales, is entirely coincidental.

Smitten With Death

COPYRIGHT © 2015 by Sharon Saracino

Cover Art by *Debbie Taylor*

The Wild Rose Press, Inc.
PO Box 708
Adams Basin, NY 14410-0708
Visit us at www.thewildrosepress.com

Publishing History
First Fantasy Rose Edition, 2015
Print ISBN 978-1-62830-822-8
Digital ISBN 978-1-62830-823-5

Max Logan Series, Book 3
Published in the United States of America

Just when I thought

I was going to make it to the bottom of my stairs agilely and uninjured, I was foiled by a conglomeration of woven gossamer strands dappled with dewdrops glinting in the sun that some eight-legged bastard had constructed between the wall of the garage and the stair railing during the night.

Have you ever noticed how walking into an unexpected spider web turns you into an instant ninja?

I slapped myself in the face, did a passable imitation of a windmill in a hurricane, and provided a short demonstration of the Argentine tango. Then I stomped the spider into a mashed splat. I left the corpse where it lay to warn off any of his friends who might have ideas of picking up where he left off and jumped the final two stairs to the sidewalk, twisting my ankle in the process. Clearing my throat, I tossed my ratty ponytail over one shoulder with a deliberate air of insouciance intended to plainly communicate to my audience that I totally meant to do that. Anyone can be good. Awesome takes practice.

Once Gail established I'd landed on my feet, as opposed to my ass—my stepmother is well acquainted with my challenged coordination—she saluted me with a grin and a white waxed-paper bag, then headed for the house to prepare the kitchen for the pending arrival of my sister and her brood. Walking slowly and rolling my hips in what I fancied was a seductive manner, in an effort to detract attention from my limp, I absently wondered if there would ever come a day when Morgan Kane would see me at my best. All things considered, it wasn't looking promising.

Praise for Sharon Saracino

Dedication

Thank you to everyone
who jumped on this crazy train from the beginning
and stayed on board for the ride!
I'm so grateful for your love and support.

Chapter 1

Normally, people who die stay that way, but to tell you the truth, I can't recall anyone ever using the word normal and the name Max Logan in the same sentence. I died and lived to tell about it. Some might argue I didn't actually die but simply enjoyed a particularly vivid Near Death Experience. Believers cite NDEs as proof of an afterlife. Scientists argue they are hallucinations of warmth, security, and light perceived as reality induced by a massive release of chemicals in the dying brain. Me? I was hardly in a position to question anyone's concept of reality. Of course, my afterlife experience was sorely lacking in warmth and security, consisting primarily of my naked butt in an unsanitary bus terminal overseen by a harried little clerk with absolutely no appreciation for my sparkling sense of humor. Thanks to my awesome ninja skills and my Kubler-Ross stages of death and dying influenced powers of persuasion, I made it back. My boyfriend and ex-husband, Roger-the-Proctologist, wasn't quite so lucky. Yeah, he's still dead. All indications are he'll be staying that way. It sucks. All. The. Time.

I'd like to believe my supernatural sojourn is behind me, but I haven't been accused of optimism in quite a while. So I hold my breath and wait for the other shoe to drop.

While waiting, I've discovered some things may be

worse than death. Like being trapped in a cramped ballroom at a wedding with two hundred and fifty or so well-meaning relatives. Most of whom still pulled a funeral face every time they glanced in my direction.

Oh, pul-eeze! Like you don't know the look I mean? Yeah, I knew you did.

"How are you *really*, dear?" Great Aunt Tess shouted the question to me over her fruit cup.

"Just living the dream, Aunt Tess."

I tapped my finger to the side of my lips hoping subtly to alert her to the thick fruit syrup dribbling from the corner of her mouth and threatening to saturate the nest of gray, stubbly whiskers sprouting from her chin. She failed to take the hint, and her face puckered into a clearly skeptical expression at my response.

Aunt Tess had embraced her widowhood with the maniacal fervor of a vegan avoiding a platter of prime rib since 1967. Every item of clothing the woman owned was unrelieved black. No doubt, my scarlet *O'Hell-no* bridesmaid gown was even more offensive to my perpetually bereaved aunt than it was to me. Albeit for entirely different reasons. The red leather jacket I'd worn to the rehearsal dinner last night probably would have induced seizures. I guess I'm just not one of those women who feels the need to advertise my loss via my wardrobe—for forty years.

"You're so brave, Maxine," she mumbled around her diced peaches. "No one knows better than me how difficult it is."

"Actually, Aunt Tess, I'm not brave at all. But I do believe one has to be practical."

Besides, I'd already tried wallowing on for size and discovered it's as useless as pants on a hooker. It simply leads to weight gain and in the end, doesn't change a thing. With a sigh, I pushed my fruit filled parfait glass over to my father, the Hardware King of Hamilton, who scraped his spoon in the bottom of his with the desperation of a starving man.

"Roger is gone. Questionable fashion choices won't bring him back."

Nothing would bring him back. I knew that better than anyone. Because I was the one who'd hunted his dead butt down in the afterlife and tried. Everyone tells me when one door closes another door opens. What no one told me is the long, lonely hallway leading to the next door is a complete and total bitch. But I was doing okay. Mostly. Though sometimes I do feel like a duck floating on a lake—smooth and calm on the surface, and paddling like hell underneath to keep from sinking.

Okay, so maybe I didn't get to choose the music, but I could damn well choose how to dance, right? Also, it wouldn't hurt if someone really *had* let me choose the music—at least for tonight. I was pretty sure even *I* could have put together a better playlist than Dancing Frankie, the five foot six, three hundred and seventy-five pound karaoke packing DJ.

Did I mention his name was Dancing Frankie? Don't even attempt a visual. I promise you couldn't do him justice. Seriously.

To add insult to injury, pink is not my color. I'm simply not a pastel kind of girl. Unlike my willowy, blonde half-sister Denise, nothing about me screams delicate and dainty. In fact, I'd hazard a guess nothing even whispers it. I'm more of a jewel tone type. I'm all about the drama.

Tell me this surprises you.

3

Still, my cousin Mary Ann had been planning this day since 1979, the golden age of pastel puffery, and apparently felt compelled to pay homage. I was pretty sure the number in the wedding party exceeded the guest list and included every cousin, sorority sister, and co-worker with whom she'd ever shared a margarita. Each of us sported a different shade of insipid. The receiving line resembled a drunken Easter Bunny's nightmare. At least good foundation garments had managed to tease a hint of actual cleavage out of my less than spectacular bosom. I take what I can get.

Stepmother Gail reached under the table to pat my knee in silent appreciation of my gallant effort at polite conversation. The seventy-two yards of taffeta and chiffon crammed in my lap thwarted her attempt. People say if you can't say something nice, you shouldn't say anything at all. Gail knows if I strictly adhered to that theory, I might never speak again. She understands me, my stepmother, though I'd never given her credit for it until recently. I guess maybe death is good for a few things, after all. I was not ordinarily known for my restraint. Or tact. In fact, some people actually think I'm a smartass. I prefer to think of it as explaining why people are idiots. It's a public service, really.

Hey, I'm working on it, okay?

A gang of white-shirted wait staff descended upon the unsuspecting wedding guests like a horde of well-organized locusts. They whisked away the fruit cups, replacing them with silver-trimmed china plates piled with mixed greens topped by ruby red grape tomatoes. They conducted the maneuver with such efficiency that my father was diving in with his spoon for another goopy mouthful of fruit cocktail before he even noticed the switch. He swapped utensils with the ease of a street magician performing sleight-of-hand and stabbed a forkful of lettuce without missing a beat. When it comes to his food, Dad is flexible like that.

Actually, I'd discovered my father is flexible in a lot of ways. Sure, he'd been slightly upset when the unholy hotness that is Morgan Kane, Hellhound Grim Reaper, brought me home the day Roger died. Okay, maybe apoplectic is a more accurate description. He was even more upset when he learned the binding, designed to protect me from my supernatural superpowers, had been snapped like a dry-rotted rubber band left too long in the corner of the junk drawer with the dust bunnies and tangled paper clips. But once he accepted it was a done deal, he ultimately concluded it was my decision whether or not to embrace my supernatural sideline. If I ever reach a decision, that is. His confidence gives me the warm fuzzies, though it has made me start monitoring him carefully for other signs of early dementia.

"You gonna eat that?" Dad arched a bushy salt and pepper brow and darted a hopeful look in the direction of my untouched salad. My stepmother rolled her eyes, pulled her own plate closer, and hunched over it like a bear guarding her cub.

"Knock yourself out, Dad. I'm saving myself for the chicken."

For the record, the chicken dinner, when it arrived, wasn't nearly as impressive as the sight of Mary Ann's new in-laws staggering onto the dance floor to perform the Chicken *Dance*. An unsteady ring of half-sloshed revelers flapping their arms and wiggling their butts

5

like poultry on crack would have been entertaining enough on its own, but when they began passing around the family heirloom, a large papier-mâché bonnet fashioned in the shape of a chicken head, I knew we had reached the epitome of wedding reception chic. What next, the Electric Slide?

Almost as though my supernatural superpowers had magically expanded to encompass precognition, which as far as I knew they hadn't, the techno-strains of that oh-so-danceable classic blared through Dancing Frankie the DJ's speakers. This resulted in a coordinated *squeeeee* from every female in attendance. Excluding me. Rumor has it I'm a bit of a nonconformist.

Don't pretend this surprises you.

But it did include, I was sad to note, my sister Denise. She jumped out of her seat next to her doting husband, Brad-the-Famous-Vascular-Surgeon, and flounced in my direction. Yes, flounced. Frankly, though my sister could give lessons in flouncing when the occasion warrants, in this case, I'm pretty sure it was unintentional. In these dresses there wasn't much else a girl could do.

"C'mon, Max." She waved her arms in the general direction of the dance floor and shouted over the din of clinking cutlery. Plastering what I hoped was a look of abject disappointment on my face, I pointed first at my sequined clutch and then in the direction of the ladies restroom.

"Sorry," I mouthed.

Her shoulders slumped. Then she perked up and headed back to her table to drag her husband, Brad-the-Famous-Vascular-Surgeon, out to the dance floor where lines of guests already gyrated in an uncoordinated manner with a complete lack of musicality. Honestly, I probably wasn't a person who should be critical of the lack of coordination in others. Level surfaces have a tendency to jump up and smack me in the face. I can also fall up stairs, get hit by parked cars, and make poles magically appear in front of me at a moment's notice. I'm just talented like that. Dancing? Yeah, not worth the risk to life and limb. Mine or anyone else's. One would expect I would have acquired a modicum of dexterity at my age, but apparently, even supernatural superheroes have limitations.

With a good deal of yanking and tugging on the part of my folks, and some creative cursing and wriggling on my part, I managed to un-cram myself from under the table. Fortunately, I didn't really have to use the facilities. I suspected a real potty break might require a crane, several handmaidens, and perhaps a hunky fireman or two just to keep the dress out of the toilet. But I meandered in the direction of the little girls' room anyway, just to give credence to my fib.

I propped myself against the wall near the ladies' room door trying to appear properly chastised, rather than amused, by the evil eye cast in my direction from the dance floor by Brad-the-Famous-Vascular-Surgeon. Brad hated dancing almost as much as I hated laundry. I felt sorry for him. Okay, not really, but I thought maybe I'd try empathy on for size and see how it fit. I grinned and blew him a kiss a mere heartbeat before a cold draft snaked along the floor and crept around my limbs, bringing with it the unmistakable taint of death. Sweat popped out on my forehead and trickled down the valley between my underwire enhanced ta-tas like

Niagara Falls after a forty-day rain. My stomach tightened and heaved. My lungs felt too small to take in air. I glanced around desperately, trying to pinpoint the source of my sudden unease. This could not be good.

Back at the table, Dad was still shoveling food into his pie hole, wedding cake and ice cream this time, and Gail had turned in her chair to watch the dancing. I couldn't help noticing she'd moved her dessert plate just beyond my father's reach. Smart woman, my stepmother. Dancing Frankie was shaking his *thang*, and every other obscenely bulging jiggly bit he possessed, in a manner threatening imminent trauma to anyone within a six-foot radius. In fact, just watching him traumatized me a little. It was not pretty. But neither was it the cause of my discomfort. Well, at least not this *particular* discomfort. No one else in the room seemed aware anything had changed, but the pall of doom weighed me down like a lead apron.

Uneasily aware I might be privy to something unseen, courtesy of my supernatural super-powers, a vague whiff of sulfur compounded my disquiet. The last time that precise stench had singed my nostrils, it was closely followed by the appearance of the thick-necked, dark-haired, massively muscular Guardian of the Gates of Hell. Of course, while evil swirled around Cerberus like the cold, dark cloud I felt invading the ballroom, I also knew he couldn't arbitrarily cross over to the land of the living. I clenched my fists in the folds of my skirt and tried to ignore my inner reptile, but my lizard brain was screaming at me to get the hell out before something really bad happened.

Oh, pul-eeze! Haven't you ever heard of the lizard brain?

The lizard brain is that lump of tissue at the base of your skull that floods you with dire adrenaline warnings whenever you feel threatened. While an Internet junkie like myself knows the lizard brain has been around forever, and existed in even the earliest land animals, most people are more familiar with it as the fight or flight response.

At the moment, I was fighting flight with everything I had no matter how insistently my little green reptile whispered in my ear. This was my family in this room. Those I loved and those I would categorically deny in public and cross the street to avoid. I couldn't just abandon them to whatever threat might be imminent.

Okay, I could, but I would almost certainly feel bad about it afterwards.

I swallowed my foreboding and hurried back to the table, my eyes darting frantically around the ballroom the entire time. If something wicked was this way coming, I wanted to be near my folks to do whatever it took to keep them safe. I was just reaching for my chair to begin the backbreaking process of cramming the miles of putrid pink prom gown under the table when a sweeter and infinitely more appealing aroma tickled my nose. Well, at least it was appealing to me. Let's see, first the chill of death and now the unmistakable scent of jelly doughnuts. It could mean only one thing. The Grim Reaper was in the house. It may have been the sound of my heart, which suddenly started beating double time, but I'm pretty sure the loud thump I heard was the other freaking shoe hitting the floor.

Chapter 2

I shoved my chair back under the table and stood behind it. It was probably a good idea to remain on my feet. All the better to run like hell. I moved behind my father's chair, alert for anything unusual beyond the awkward drunken revelry surrounding me. Gail glanced up briefly and then did a double take.

"Max, honey, are you okay?" she asked. "Your complexion is the color of pea soup."

Wucking fonderful! Another color that didn't flatter me in the least. Pretty soon I'd be forced to beat the would-be suitors off with a stick. My father swiveled in his chair, a forkful of cake frozen halfway to his mouth and eyes opened wide. He swallowed hard and his brows jumped up into his receding hairline where they hung precariously like crooked crescent moons while he carefully returned the fork to his plate. He looked about as uneasy as I felt. Maybe I was wearing an expression he recognized from back in the day. The day when my mother was still alive, that is. Then again, maybe he'd finally stuffed himself to the point of no return.

It seems my mother possessed supernatural DNA, which had been inherited by yours truly. Frankly, I would have been a lot happier with the slender waist or the ample bosom gene. Coupled with the fact I'd also been blessed with my father's less than attractive feet, I was definitely splashing around in the shallow end of the family gene pool.

But I digress.

When I finally learned the truth, I also discovered my father had known about my paranormal proclivities all along but decided to ignore the entire matter as he and my mother had taken pains to have my powers bound for all eternity before she died.

One would think that was the end of it. Well, one would be wrong.

Don't sweat it. It happens to me all the time.

I am, if you can believe it—and frankly, even if you can't—a Retriever.

I will pause here briefly while you giggle. Go ahead. Get it out of your system. I had pretty much the same reaction myself. Finished?

All righty then, let's continue. I was not the canine variety with the big, soulful eyes and the soft floppy ears. My breed of Retriever is the poor schmuck variety—the one who hightails it into the afterlife when someone else screws up and retrieves the poor souls who don't belong there and returns them to their bodies.

Awesome, huh?

Believe me I wasn't especially impressed either. Imagine my surprise when I discovered the American Kennel Club doesn't even have a pedigree for *this* puppy.

My first and only retrieval thus far produced mixed results. Actually, I'd managed to retrieve the soul I was sent to snare. But despite my most heroic attempt, I hadn't been able to save Roger. After the fact, I learned I was never intended to save him in the first place. I was simply being given the chance to say good-bye.

Everyone said this was some great gift, which in hindsight, I suppose it was, but it sure hadn't seemed that way at the time. It felt as though the entire supernatural community had conspired deliberately to misinform me.

It still doesn't sit well. And though I don't blame him personally, I haven't taken any of the Grim Reaper's calls in months. Not even when I was thinking about him more frequently than I thought I should. Not even when the beautiful potted dogwood showed up on my porch on Christmas morning. He cultivates them himself. Kind of a strange hobby for a Hellhound Grim Reaper I suppose, but what's more amazing is the fact the damn thing is not only still living, it's truly thriving. In my house. This might not seem to be a big deal, but on those rare occasions when I decide to tempt fate and consider filling my apartment, better known as the Plant Cemetery, with lush greenery, I always manage to select plants with no will to live. Sadly, some have even felt obliged to commit suicide in my car on the way home. Plants and I are not friends. Just saying.

"Is something wrong?" Dad whispered out of the side of his mouth, gangster style.

"I'm not sure." Apparently, even ignoring Death's phone calls wasn't enough to keep him away indefinitely. My eyes continued to scan the room but nothing seemed out of the ordinary. Well, except for the big chicken head still bobbing through the crowd. I'm sure that isn't considered ordinary anywhere.

Finally, I spotted him lounging with one massive shoulder holding up the wall at the back of the ballroom. He was huge. He was hot. He was wearing a big, black cape so I couldn't see for sure, but I had no doubt he still had a great ass. He was Morgan Kane, Hellhound Grim Reaper.

Oddly, his wicked scars seemed less pronounced than when I'd last seen him. The hood of his cloak hid his long, dark hair, but his eyes were just as green, so green I could discern their color even from this side of the room. I felt as though they were boring right into my soul as he stared across the distance between us. Sometimes he's kind of intense like that.

The corner of his mouth quirked up in a lopsided grin when he realized I'd spotted him. I gathered up the unwieldy layers of my skirt and stomped across the floor in his direction. I had no idea who he was here for, but I wondered if there was any way I could play the guilt card and persuade him to deviate from his schedule for at least a couple of hours.

"Logan." He nodded pleasantly as I pulled up short, less than six inches from his chest. He inclined his head slightly and looked down his nose at me. No great accomplishment on his part. He was well over six and half feet tall, and I wouldn't be considered statuesque anywhere, except perhaps in Munchkinland. Assuming I was wearing heels. And standing on a crate.

What? God only lets things grow until they're perfect and some of us simply didn't take as long.

"Kane," I hissed through my pasted on grin. "What in the hell are you doing here?"

"Gee, Logan, it's nice to see you, too," he sighed. "If you would answer a phone call once in a while, I might not have to resort to showing up unexpectedly at family functions to get your attention."

"If I didn't answer your call, it's probably because I was singing along with my ringtone and got carried away," I sniffed.

It happens.

"Besides, it's not like you don't know where I live."

I wasn't trying to be insolent, but it's often the way I react to terror. The arrival of the Grim Reaper at anyone's wedding was probably not the most auspicious way to start a marriage.

Before he had a chance to respond, my third cousin Fred shuffled up behind me.

"Maxine, are you okay?"

"I'm fine," I lied. "Why?"

I realize some people might perceive Morgan Kane with his black cape, immense size, and unearthly green eyes as a threat. I, on the other hand, found him incredibly appealing. Which I refuse to examine too closely. Nonetheless, I couldn't believe Fred was tactless enough to ask me if I was okay right in front of the man.

"Well." Fred shifted from one foot to the other. "You're standing here talking to the wall."

"I'm..." I closed my eyes and counted to ten. Then I opened them and glared at Kane.

"Guess I should have mentioned no one except you can see me at the moment." He grinned.

Thinking quickly—*What? It happens*—I tapped the side of my head near my ear.

"Phone," I mouthed, shrugging at Fred.

"Oh! Right. Sorry, didn't mean to interrupt." He scurried away, glancing over his shoulder every few feet as though he wasn't quite sure whether to or not to believe me.

"So," I asked in the most nonchalant tone I could

muster, as soon as Fred had moved a safe distance away. "What are you doing here?"

"I wanted to talk to you."

"And it couldn't have waited until...oh, I don't know... *never*? Seriously, Kane, couldn't it at least wait until after the wedding? You showing up here is going to give my father a coronary, and you promised he wasn't on your list anytime soon."

"He's not. What's wrong, Logan? You're all flushed. In fact, right at the moment, your face almost matches your dress. Nice look, by the way. Haven't seen that particular style in...hmm, actually, I'm not sure I've ever seen that particular style."

"If you must know, this dress makes me feel like a sparkly princess," I retorted with a haughty toss of my head.

He didn't seem convinced, either.

Anyway, I was pretty sure he was wrong about my face matching my dress. Based on the level of heat baking my cheeks, I suspected I was sporting an unbecoming shade of scarlet rather than the soft petal pink of my voluminous skirt.

"Yeah, you should go with that. And for future reference, pink is not your color."

"Says the guy in the big black cape of doom. Who are you, the Fashion Police? You packing a scythe under there, too?"

"Maybe." He laughed.

"So you just dropped by to stoke the fires of my raging self-consciousness?"

"Actually, Logan, I'm here on a tip, trying to head off a problem. The tip didn't pan out, and I realized you were here, so I figured it was a good opportunity to talk to you."

"Really? Then what's with the cloak?" I plucked at the layers of black fabric swirling around him. Not that he wasn't a sight to behold, but personally, I thought the cloak covered way too much. In a tight pair of jeans, Morgan Kane was downright drool-worthy. Not that I'd noticed.

"Well, it *is* a formal occasion." He shrugged those massively broad shoulders.

The bright and witty retort on the tip of my tongue dissolved into thin air, replaced by a panicked stutter the moment I heard the scream. A small knot of people had gathered on the opposite side of the dance floor, and I saw Brad-the-Famous-Vascular-Surgeon shouldering his way through the crowd until he reached the center. This could not be good. Throwing a dark look in Kane's direction, I hiked up my skirt and ran.

When I finally elbowed my way to the center of the circle, the man lying face up on the floor with wide, staring eyes and a rapidly mottling face wasn't anyone I knew. Must be someone from the groom's side. Thank God! Then I realized how selfish that was. It might not be anyone I knew, but it was someone somebody here knew…and probably loved.

"Kane you somabitch, she's been planning this wedding since 1979," I shouted at the ceiling. "Don't you dare pull this crap now. A couple of hours either way won't cause the universe to implode." The stunned wedding guests clustered in a circle around us regarded me oddly.

Oops! Did I say that out loud? My bad.

"Oh…and um, God bless us, every one." I bowed my head and improvised quickly. A smattering of puzzled amens punctuated the air. Apparently you really could fool some of the people some of the time. Who knew?

I dropped to my knees across from Brad, which caused my hoop skirt to lever up in the back, exposing my miscellanea to all and sundry. No doubt, Morgan Kane had a dandy view from where he was standing. Of course, he'd seen it all before. In fact, he hadn't simply seen it, he'd also laundered it when, in a frozen stupor, I peed myself on the occasion of our first meeting.

Hey, it's a body's natural reaction to hypothermia, okay?

The vessels in the extremities constrict and force the fluid to the core to conserve heat. The kidneys start working overtime to process the fluid…it's got to go somewhere. Do I know how to make a first impression, or what? Yeah, story of my life. Anyway, I was over the mortification. Mostly. At least they'd been *nice* panties.

Brad had already loosened the guy's tie and was feeling for a pulse while calmly directing the bystanders to elevate the victim's legs and call 911. His eyes met mine over the afflicted man's chest.

"I've got a pulse, but he's not breathing," Brad shared in a hushed voice, no doubt hoping to avoid a panic. "I'll start rescue breathing. Can you monitor his pulse and let me know if it stops?"

I nodded mutely and pressed two fingers to the guy's neck, sliding them to the side of his windpipe and feeling for his carotid artery while Brad moved to his head and tipped it back, thrusting the jaw forward. Just as Brad was about to seal his lips around those of the stricken man and administer the breath of life, a voice as deep and smooth as dark chocolate whispered next to my ear, ruffling my hair and suffusing my entire being with heat.

"Olive."

"What?"

"Jerry's been guzzling dirty martinis like there's no tomorrow. 'Course if you don't get that olive out of his windpipe, there won't be for him. I'd suggest abdominal thrusts."

My head jerked up so fast I feared I'd given myself whiplash. I cranked my head first to the left and then to the right. No one was there. Naturally. Oh, what the hell. If the Grim Reaper offers you an out, it's best to go with the flow. I bunched up my skirt and threw my leg over Jerry's hips like a drunken cowgirl mounting a mechanical bull. If the look Brad-the-Famous-Vascular-Surgeon shot in my direction was any indication, I wasn't alone in thinking I might be crazy.

"One word, Bradley, and I will personally hunt down and burn every single pair of cashmere socks you own," I threatened darkly. An expression of reluctant fear crept into his face. My brother-in-law, Brad-the-Famous-Vascular-Surgeon, has a peculiar attachment to his cashmere socks. The socks are black. He wears them every day. Even in the summer. With sandals. It is not an attractive look. My sister Denise and I have conspired against him for years. We've switched out his sock drawer, and we've hidden his sandals. We have achieved limited success. Okay, so maybe we've accomplished squat. He clings to those damn socks with the determination of a baby holding onto its security blanket.

I curled my right hand and set the heel of my fist in

the region of Jerry's solar plexus topping it with my left. I shifted my weight forward, pressing in and upward with everything I had. Nothing happened. I took a deep, fortifying breath and tried again.

"What in the hell are you doing?" My brother-in-law whispered furiously.

"Olive." I gasped, rocking back and burying my fist in Jerry's gut for the third time.

"Huh?"

"I said…" I grunted breathlessly. I tried to shift my position and get up on my knees for added power, but lost my balance entirely—*surprise*—which then caused me to pitch forward and jam my elbows in Jerry's midsection to catch myself in lieu of a fourth thrust. There was a muted pop and a squeal of air that reminded me of a deflating balloon. Jerry coughed once and a large green olive shot out of his mouth with the force of a bullet, smacking Brad-the-Famous-Vascular-Surgeon right between the eyes. "It's an olive."

I sat back and dragged my forearm across my moist brow, trembling. Surely, it was due to anxiety and exertion. Kane's bone melting voice and hot breath on the side of my neck had absolutely nothing to do with it. Nope, not a thing.

"Max? What were you thinking?" Brad bellowed.

I gestured to the puddle of ice and shattered glass near my knee. "It occurred to me Jerry had one martini too many and may have choked on an olive."

Quick thinker. That's me.

Of course, it doesn't exactly hurt to have a little afterlife assistance, either.

"What if it wasn't, Maxine? What if you were wrong, and he was having a cardiac event?" Brad climbed to his feet and reached a hand down to pull me to mine.

"But it was, and he wasn't. Honestly, I don't know why you're getting so upset with me for being right. I'm not the least bit upset with you for being wrong." I shrugged, patted his cheek, and offered him an innocent smile. Then I disentangled my fingers from his to tug my skirt back into place. Brad opened his mouth to respond. Then he seemed to remember who he was dealing with and settled for rolling his eyes before turning to direct the paramedics wheeling a litter into the ballroom.

Jerry was still coughing and sputtering on the floor but had managed to take in enough oxygen to request another martini and make it clear he was loudly and vocally opposed to a scenic side trip to the emergency room.

"Look, pal," Brad-the-Famous-Vascular-Surgeon said, squatting next to the man, exposing a flash of his oh-so-sexy socks, and rocking his best Ivy League School of Medicine voice. "It's always better to get checked out in these situations. If even a small piece of olive managed to get down into your lungs, you could end up with a vegetative pneumonia. Now, you don't want that to happen, do you?"

The stricken man's eyes widened, and he slowly shook his head from side to side like a hypnotized puppet. I was sure he had no idea what vegetative pneumonia was, but when Brad-the-Famous-Vascular-Surgeon delivered the threat in that particularly doctor-ish tone, he sure made it sound like something a guy didn't want to mess around with.

I staggered back to my table and grabbed the

pitcher of ice water, which was sweating a big wet ring onto the tablecloth next to the crookedly melting candlelit centerpiece. Barely resisting the urge to dump it over my head, I sloshed a generous portion into my glass and chugged it down. Swallow, fill, repeat.

"Is everything okay, Max?" Dad's brows drew together like a thick, fuzzy caterpillar burrowed into the pleats in his forehead.

Drawing in a deep breath, I looked around slowly. I was no longer sweating, nor could I detect a hint of either sulfur or jelly doughnuts. Whatever his real reason for crashing my cousin's wedding, Morgan Kane had apparently left the building. Crisis averted. For now, at least.

"I hope so, Daddy. I sure hope so."

Chapter 3

I'm pretty sure I'd like mornings a whole lot better if they occurred at a more convenient time of the day. It had been one of those nights where sleep had been so elusive I suspected the limited capacity of my coffee pot might not be up to the challenge of jumpstarting my brain. In desperation, at two o'clock this morning, I'd even tried taking a little plastic cupful of that nighttime coughing, sneezing, stuffy head, oh my God there's a freakin' dragon under the bed medicine. Yeah, I won't be doing that again anytime soon. I was seriously contemplating the idea of just filling the sink with coffee, dunking in my head, and opening my mouth. Attractive? No. Effective? Questionable, at best. I settled for brewing a second pot.

Coffee slut that I am, I pulled the carafe out to refill my Mornings are Not Pretty mug before the brew cycle was complete. The sizzle of liquid on the hot element and the sad, distinctive aroma of burnt java filled my open plan kitchen-office-fine dining area. Note to self—the Bible says thou shalt not waste the coffee. Okay, maybe it isn't the Bible, maybe it's the gospel according to that South American farmer and his coffee bean bearing burro, Paquito.

Yes, I have named the donkey. A little compassion would not be unwelcome here. Addiction is an illness, people.

My very independent and morbidly obese cat, Sir Chicken Caesar finally decided to emerge from the bedroom. He arrogantly strutted—okay, he awkwardly waddled—across the expanse of the living room and collapsed at my feet wearing an expression that clearly asked, "Where's my breakfast, biotch?" With a sigh, I retrieved two cans from the pantry cabinet and held them up for his inspection. He sniffed the air, then daintily licked a paw and began to wash his face. Okay, then. Apparently, he was leaving the choice up to me. As I popped the ring tab and dumped a gelled and foul smelling portion of tuna surprise into his blue pottery dish, I pondered the reason for the sudden reappearance of my insomnia. Honestly, it didn't take a rocket scientist to figure it out. After tactfully leaving me to my grief for what they considered an acceptable period of time, the supernatural community had apparently decided my sabbatical was over. Why is it every time I think I've got my shit together, some fool comes along and flushes the toilet?

I mean, c'mon. I died, came back, filled in for the Superintendent of Spiritual Impediment aka SSI, successfully resolved the unfinished business of the reluctantly deceased, and learned a whole lot about myself in the process. One would think that should be enough for any one person to experience in a lifetime. One would think that would be the end of it.

One would, as you may have already suspected, be wrong.

Just when I thought it was safe to chalk my entire untimely demise up to a rather creative hallucination brought about by a nasty knock on the head and an unhealthy dependence on commercially prepared convenience food, Alicia, the SSI, showed up in the middle of the night. Glowing like a nuclear reactor, she informed me I was, in fact, a supernatural super-being and it was time to put on my shiny cape and twinkling tiara and hoof it on over to the Grim Reaper's place. Time to learn how to venture into the afterlife to retrieve souls. Not only wasn't I provided with an instruction manual or quart-sized travel mug of coffee for the road, I got caught in a blizzard. Then I hit a tree, nearly froze to death, and was ultimately rescued by a renegade Hellhound in the person of Morgan Kane, the Grim Reaper. A Grim Reaper who launders panties, makes a mean cup of Joe, cultivates dogwood trees, and is hotter than a billy goat's ass in a pepper patch. And people say I need a hobby. Seriously? When exactly am I supposed to pencil in an origami class?

Bottom line? I hadn't been able to retrieve my ex-husband, Roger-the-Proctologist from the afterlife. Sure, realistically I understood that knowing in advance, retrieving him was never the intention, wouldn't have changed anything. But reasonable or not, I was still pouting about the injustice of it all. Woman's prerogative, right? If it's true that what doesn't kill you makes you stronger, I figure I should be able to bench press the entire defensive line of the Hamilton High School Porcupines by now.

I snagged my coffee cup, stuffed my arms into a hoodie, wandered across the living room to the French doors, and let myself out onto my small, covered deck. I left the door open a crack in case Caesar decided to lower his standards enough to join me. I had no expectation he would. After all, I was just the staff.

I set my steaming mug on the flat arm of one of the

two hulking Adirondack chairs that took up the lion's share of the space and lowered myself into the seat. Despite my ongoing resolution, I still hadn't taken the time to scrape and paint the peeling wood, and loose paint flecks poked my legs as I settled myself. Maybe I could just buy some nice cushions? I propped my bare feet on the railing and stared out at the woods behind the house. It sure as hell beat staring at my bare feet propped on the railing. Given it was late March in Pennsylvania, socks may have been a wise choice.

Perhaps I've mentioned I have my father's feet?

Well, in case I haven't, I do, and I try to keep them covered at all times. There isn't a pedicure or a cute pair of sandals on the planet that can totally disguise the fugly.

I sipped my coffee and clung to the brief serenity of the morning. It wouldn't last. Nothing ever did, so I'd learned to take what I could get when I could get it. I listened to the sweet trill of morning birdsong and tried hard to concentrate on anything other than the reason Morgan Kane had unexpectedly appeared at my cousin's wedding. I might have had more success in not thinking about him if the potted dogwood he'd sent hadn't been sitting in the corner of the deck daring me to ignore it. I swear the damn thing mocked me just by its survival. Hence the reason it was outside on the deck.

When I'd met Granny-Apple-Head, aka the Timekeeper, in the Between during the course of my unsuccessful foray into the Great Beyond to save Roger, she told me that according to legend, the dogwood flower is a symbol of healing and sacrifice. A plant that appears fragile but with a stem that's tough and resilient, resistant to damage. In other words, it bends, but it doesn't break. I hadn't understood the significance at the time. After all, I was on a mission and said mission did not include lessons in horticulture. Then Roger had said the same thing about me as I stood before him facing the reality of his loss with my heart shattered, unsure I could withstand the grief. I bend, but I don't break. I hadn't believed him. Actually, I hadn't given the comparison much actual thought until I returned home the night before Roger's funeral and found a vase of dogwood waiting for me.

Have I mentioned supernatural and subtle are apparently incapable of co-existing?

Admittedly, at the time I'd both needed and welcomed the reminder. I'd also needed and welcomed the bottle of gin the Grim Reaper had left along with it. I'm not sure whether or not he intended it for medicinal purposes, but it'd sure cured what ailed me for a couple of hours. And the resultant crying jag left me feeling refreshed, restored, and ready to face a new day. Yeah.

In any event, it turned out everyone was right. I'd bent nearly in half, but I didn't break. I survived. Sure, it still hurt, but I'm healing. I'm moving on. It's what Roger had wanted, and to be clear, I didn't have much of a choice. I was getting all my ducks in a row. I took a big slug of java to wash down the uneasy feeling that the sudden reappearance of the Grim Reaper in my life was the prelude to open season on ducks. Given my history, it seemed a reasonable assumption.

Hey, I said my outlook was improving, I never claimed I'd attained the rank of cock-eyed optimist.

I heard the unmistakable crunch of tires on gravel and realized Dad and Gail must already be home from church. It meant I'd been sitting here far longer than I thought, and the Logan family Sunday morning post-church coffee klatch was imminent. The get-together was an unofficially scheduled event that never varied. Attendance was mandatory. For a long time, I'd avoided all that one-big-happy-family groove by showing up late, wolfing down a bagel, and slugging back a cup of Joe just in time for the entire affair to break up. I'd embraced my black-sheep status with open arms and a complete limited-edition collection of defense mechanisms, certain every moment I spent with my family was a moment I was being judged. And I was. But it turned out I was the lone member of the jury. Everyone else was simply tiptoeing around me, trying to figure out how to get close. Yeah, self-sabotage and I are old friends.

These days, I usually had the kitchen set up and ready to roll by the time Dad and Gail pulled in with the baked goods, and well before Denise, Brad-the-Famous-Vascular-Surgeon, the terrible twosome, Mick and Vick, and Clinique, the howling wonder-dog arrived.

Yes, my sister named her dog after a cosmetic company.

I tossed back my last shot of coffee, indulged in a jaw cracking yawn, and dropped my fugly feet back to the deck. I must have been more preoccupied than I thought to have so completely lost track of time.

I shuffled back inside and gave my coffee cup a quick rinse in the sink, leaving it next to the coffee pot. I find it saves time in an emergency. You know, like a sudden life-threatening drop in my caffeine level. As I skipped toward my bedroom to get dressed…Okay, perhaps I didn't skip exactly. In fact, I don't skip. I'm not that coordinated. I actually paused to glance out the window. There was Dad's beat up blue pick-up with Logan's Hardware stenciled in white on the door, there was Roger's luxury German SUV, which had replaced my poor ten-year-old Ford, and there was Morgan Kane's impressively decked out fire-engine red four by four. My stomach began to churn with the force of the heavy-duty cycle on an industrial washing machine. My family was due to arrive any minute, and the Grim Reaper was sitting in the driveway with rock music blaring through the open windows. Wucking fonderful!

Despite my apprehension, I couldn't stop my lips from twitching as the song ended and I heard the distinctive opening strains of "Don't Fear the Reaper." Like me, Morgan Kane had obviously graduated from the American Academy of Subtlety. I had to hand it to him, the guy knew how to make an entrance. At least he'd ditched the cape today. The morning temperature was a hovering in the low forties, and he was wearing nothing but flannel, so maybe that whole being a Hellhound thing gave him some peculiar ability to generate his own heat. I know being around him had a tendency to jack my temperature up a couple of degrees.

Kane's fingers tapped on the steering wheel in time to the music. He stared straight ahead and didn't appear to be in any great hurry to hike up the stairs to my door.

If you've ever seen my stairs, you'd understand why.

Although he may have conquered Everest, I suspect even Sir Edmund Hillary might have thought twice about tackling the ascent to my place. Thankful for small favors, I sprinted into the bedroom to throw on some clothes.

I'm pretty sure my high school gym teacher would have been awestruck by the agility I exhibited in hurdling my cat who lay sprawled out in a patch of sunlight in the middle of the living room floor. Sir Chicken Caesar was less than impressed. He rolled over with an irritated grunt at my audacity in disturbing his nap. It takes a lot more than a sudden burst of coordination to excite my feline. In fact, in fourteen years, I'm not sure I've discovered anything that does. Perhaps if I hung Maryland Crab Cakes from my ass and did the Macarena?

Since I'd planned to schlep next door in my oversized sleep shirt, a pair of flannel lounge pants, and some pink bunny slippers, I hadn't bothered to peruse my available wardrobe. Sadly, my available wardrobe currently consisted of one pair of jeans and a wrinkled blue sweatshirt. My unavailable wardrobe consisted of nearly every other item of clothing I own. Remember how you felt when you found out Santa Claus wasn't real? Well, that's pretty much how I felt when I discovered there was no Laundry Fairy. Still, every morning I wake up and look at that laundry basket with hope in my heart, doomed to endure the crush of disappointment yet again. My laundry avoidance skills are epic.

I quickly threaded my arms and legs through my awesome fashion finds and turned to regard my reflection in the full-length mirror on the back of the bathroom door. Why is it that the image of myself I have in my head bears so little resemblance to the one in the mirror? Gravity is a heartless bitch. Everyone knows mirrors don't lie. Most days I'm simply thankful they don't laugh.

With one ear cocked for the slam of Kane's truck door and the other wide open for the crunch of my stepmother's compact pulling into the drive, I quickly combed my fingers through my hair, wincing at the painful tugs on my scalp when they snagged in the tousled waves. It was uncomfortably stiff with the residual hairspray required to hold it in the elaborate up-do my cousin Mary Ann insisted on for the wedding party participants, yesterday.

I didn't have the energy for a shower by the time I got home and wasn't planning on seeing anyone other than my immediate family first thing this morning, so I thought I was safe. My loved ones know better than to expect much from me on Sunday mornings.

I finally gathered the whole tragic mess into an untidy ponytail and secured it with an elastic band. Why I was so worried about my appearance, anyway, I don't know. It wasn't as if the Grim Reaper hadn't already seen me at my worst. Cyanosis and incontinence? Shouldn't be too hard to improve on that kind of first impression.

I gripped the hem of my shirt and tugged it down over my hips hoping to stretch out a few of the wrinkles. As soon as I released the tension, it sprang back into creases, just like an accordion. Lovely. Thus, cleverly disguised as a semi-responsible adult, I took a deep breath and headed for the door while mentally bracing myself for my second encounter with the Grim Reaper in less than twenty-four hours.

Chapter 4

Pausing to take a deep breath and blow it out again, I clenched my teeth and flung open the door. The sight that met my eyes made me want to scoop them out with a melon-baller. I try to be a "glass half-full" kind of girl. Unfortunately, some fool keeps slapping the damn glass out of my hand before I even get the chance to take a sip.

There in the driveway, my father was shaking hands and chatting semi-amicably with Morgan Kane. Furthermore, Gail was waving the white waxed-paper bags in front of his face in a tempting manner that indicated she was inviting him in for coffee.

If anyone asks what's for breakfast? Death and doughnuts, I guess.

With three sets of eyes glued to my sadly rumpled form, I began a graceful descent from my one bedroom over garage. After Roger died, I'd given serious consideration to keeping the condo. I'd even tried it on for size for a week. In seven days and nights, I never once dunked my bare ass in the toilet in the middle of the night because the seat was left up, my toothpaste was always squeezed from the bottom of the tube, and I didn't find a single toenail clipping in the bathroom sink. Funny how someone's quirky little habits that set your teeth on edge day after day when you live with them are the very things you miss most when they're gone. Yeah, that. Bottom line? It just wasn't the same, and I decided torturing myself wasn't worth it simply to acquire additional square footage and upgrade my zip code. Besides, I also discovered, surprisingly I wasn't really that girl anymore.

Just when I thought I was going to make it to the bottom of my stairs agilely and uninjured, I was foiled by a conglomeration of woven gossamer strands dappled with dewdrops glinting in the sun that some eight-legged bastard had constructed between the wall of the garage and the stair railing during the night.

Have you ever noticed how walking into an unexpected spider web turns you into an instant ninja?

I slapped myself in the face, did a passable imitation of a windmill in a hurricane, and provided a short demonstration of the Argentine tango. Then I stomped the spider into a mashed splat. I left the corpse where it lay to warn off any of his friends who might have ideas of picking up where he left off and jumped the final two stairs to the sidewalk, twisting my ankle in the process. Clearing my throat, I tossed my ratty ponytail over one shoulder with a deliberate air of insouciance intended to plainly communicate to my audience that I totally meant to do that. Anyone can be good. Awesome takes practice.

Once Gail established I'd landed on my feet, as opposed to my ass—my stepmother is well acquainted with my challenged coordination—she saluted me with a grin and a white waxed-paper bag, then headed for the house to prepare the kitchen for the pending arrival of my sister and her brood. Walking slowly and rolling my hips in what I fancied was a seductive manner, in an effort to detract attention from my limp, I absently wondered if there would ever come a day when Morgan Kane would see me at my best. All things considered, it wasn't looking promising.

"You okay, kid?" Dad asked as I approached. I deliberately ignored the way Kane's lips twitched while he struggled to maintain what I assumed was supposed to be a concerned expression. For the record, he was failing miserably.

"Fine, Dad." I shifted my attention to the Grim Reaper. "What are you doing here?"

"I told you last night, I wanted to talk to you." At least he'd left the cloak and scythe at home this morning or, at the very least, in his truck. Of course, the way the black tee stretched tautly under the flannel shirt accentuated the heavy muscles of his broad chest. I didn't even want to think about the appeal of the faded denim molded lovingly to his rather fine ass. This morning's ensemble made me even more nervous than his official work garb did for reasons I chose not to dwell upon too closely, at the moment.

"About?" I prompted, feeling relatively secure in the knowledge that whatever his business, he wouldn't discuss it in front of my father.

"The stages of psychosocial development," he announced with a smug grin. It was then I noticed both corners of his mouth curled up. His scars were nearly gone. A faint white discoloration remained to assure me they'd actually been there, but the difference was astounding. Intellectually, I knew it was impossible. He'd been attacked by Cerberus, his distant Hellhound cousin and the Guardian of the Gates of Hell, while attempting to rescue his sister Alia. The battle had left wicked scars on his face and torso, not to mention half of his ear had been torn away. Realistically there was no way in Hell, or anyplace else I was aware of, scars of that magnitude could magically disappear. Then again, any preconceived notions I may have had about reality were shot to hell the day I died, and any others I might have been clinging to have continued to crumble like stale cookies in the interim.

My father cleared his throat, and sudden heat rushed into my cheeks. Yeah, okay, I'd been staring. I mean, seriously, the guy was hot in ways that had nothing to do with his being spawned in the suburbs of Hell. Worse, the Grim Reaper clearly knew I'd been staring, and his smile stretched even wider. Bad doggie.

"Ho, ho, ho," Dad chuckled like a demented Santa. "You've got the wrong sister, Kane. Denise is the psychology aficionado."

Damn! Denise. How was I going to explain Morgan Kane to my inquisitive and annoyingly perceptive sister? Let them say what they will about blondes, Denise's mind is a steel trap. She would remember Kane from the brief glimpse she'd had of him when he brought me home the day Roger died. Furthermore, she would also recall my lame explanation that he was merely a stranger who worked at the garage where I'd had the car towed. And now, out of the blue, he was included in the family coffee klatch? No doubt about it, an uncomfortable interrogation was imminent.

"Psychology junkie is more accurate," I grumbled irritably. If there was a psychology class offered anywhere within a fifty mile radius, my sister's was the first name on the roster. She never did anything with all of those college credits she accumulated, and I doubted she ever would. I guess she simply felt compelled to understand what made people tick. She frequently, and irksomely, pulled some deep insight out of her bottomless designer bag of tricks to explain my behavior to me. Just because she was often spot on didn't make it any less irritating. On the contrary.

"I guess everybody's got their vices." Dad laughed. "Well, I'd better get into the house and give Gail a hand. See you inside." Dad nodded politely at Kane and loped off in the direction of the back door, leaving an awkward lapse in conversation in his wake.

"Sooooo…" I buried my clenched fists in my pockets and pretended to be engrossed in the artistic pattern I was tracing in the gravel of the drive with the toe of my tennis shoe.

"So?" I hated the fact that such an innocuous word, when spoken in the deep, smoky voice of the Grim Reaper, had the power to make me press my thighs together and squirm. I made the mistake of looking up and meeting those piercing green eyes, and the sensation became even more pronounced. It should be illegal for Death to look so good.

"What are you really doing here?" I choked out, dreading the answer. No doubt, some denizen of the supernatural realm had screwed up yet again, and I was going to be asked to skip on over to the Between and haul someone's mostly dead ass back to the land of the living.

"Were you not paying attention, Logan? I told you I wanted to discuss developmental psychology."

"Yeah, I was paying attention, but just because I'm awake does not mean I'm functional. It's the weekend. My brain doesn't start firing on all cylinders until at least noon," I shot back.

"I see." Kane smirked. I found myself fascinated with the way his well-formed lips moved.

Did I mention his scars were pretty much gone, and his face was now whole, perfect, and incredibly beautiful?

And he had his long, dark hair pulled back in a low ponytail that offered an unobstructed view of his flawlessness? Yeah.

"And here I thought you'd be all bright-eyed and bushy tailed at ten forty-five in the morning."

"If you want bright-eyed and bushy tailed, get yourself a pet squirrel." I was relieved to discover that even my odd fascination with Morgan Kane's beauty did not render me speechless. Then again, if my family had an opinion, they'd say no one had yet discovered anything that could. "And now that you've gotten yourself invited for coffee, would you care to enlighten me as to how I'm supposed to explain you?"

"Explain me?" His brow wrinkled in a look of genuine confusion.

I eyed him critically. Given his overwhelming gorgeousness, Denise *might* buy I'd had a moment of temporary insanity leading to an uncharacteristic one-night stand after the wedding. It would be a bonus if she thought I possessed the talent to seduce such a stunning man on my own.

"Is there an echo out here? Yes, explain you. I can't exactly announce the Grim Reaper just happened to drop by for doughnuts and psychobabble."

It might even persuade Denise to cease and desist her persistent efforts to set me up with one of Brad-the-Famous-Vascular-Surgeon's golf buddies. *Score!*

Sometimes my own brilliance astounds me. I opened my mouth to ascertain whether Morgan Kane would agree to play along with my clever ruse, but his next words stopped me cold.

"Sure you can, Logan. Hell, everyone but your nieces knows the truth."

"What?" Damn, it was going to be a real challenge to consume the freshly fried doughnut stuffed with raspberry jam and topped with thick white frosting and coconut awaiting my attention on my father's kitchen table with my jaw dragging on the ground like this. Kane hooked two long, calloused fingers under my chin, and snapped my mouth shut. My eyebrows, however, remained buried somewhere in the region of my hairline.

"Your father contacted me a couple of months ago to find out if telling your family the truth violated any preternatural rules." He shrugged and let his hand fall back to his side.

"Huh?"

You may have already recognized the fact I am frequently mistaken for the Queen of Witty Repartee.

"He figured it would make your life a bit easier if you didn't have to hide who and what you are from the people closest to you."

"And does it?" I whispered in a shaky voice, grabbing the front of his shirt in a tight fist and yanking him down to my eye level.

"Well, how should I know, Logan? You tell me," he replied irritably, plucking my fist from his shirt and straightening to his full, intimidating, six and half foot height.

"No," I shook my head. "I mean, does it violate the

rules?" The squirrels in my head were doing a frenetic salsa. What if telling the others had landed my father on some heavenly hit list?

"Probably." Kane shrugged again. I wondered if he was doing it on purpose to draw attention to the magnificent breadth of his shoulders. I mean, it was, you know, working and all, but still..."Hey, I'm not planning on telling anyone. You?"

"Well, duh!" The overwhelming sense of relief I felt at knowing my father wasn't about to be hauled off to some Court of the Damned was short-lived. Gravel crunched behind me, and my sister's sparkling blue BMW X5 luxury SUV hummed into the drive.

"God help me," I whispered mournfully. "Yenta has arrived."

"Are you referring to an old busybody in general or a matchmaker in particular?" The Grim Reaper's piercing green eyes crinkled in amusement as he looked over my head for the source of the unremitting howls emanating from my sister's dog, Clinique.

Given the eardrum-perforating cacophony coming from my sister's vehicle, I could fully appreciate the fact my brother-in-law, Brad-the-Famous-Vascular-Surgeon, preferred to drive his own car. Oh sure, he always says he's on call and might have to leave unexpectedly, but just between us, I'm pretty sure it was the most plausible excuse he could think of to steal fifteen minutes of peace and quiet.

"Both? So, okay it's the blonde, blue-eyed, Catholic version in great shoes," I conceded. "But the method to her madness is the same."

I figured it was going to take Denise at least another two to three minutes to harness the dog, gather

Mick and Vick the chattering twins, and herd them all from the car and into the house. I knew with complete certainty the moment my sister's baby blues got a gander at the awesome hotness that was Morgan Kane, her mission would be clear. The only thing scarier than a best-selling horror novel was my sister in matchmaker mode. I was doomed.

"Reaper, I need a favor," I choked out and cleared my throat.

"Sure, Logan." His gaze came back to rest on my face. "What can I do for you?"

"Um, kiss me?" I squeaked as my face heated with the fire of a thousand desert suns.

"Huh?" Judging by the expression on his face, whatever favor Morgan Kane had been anticipating, locking lips with the crazy woman hadn't even made his list.

"Look," I whispered in a rush after glancing back to confirm Denise had almost gotten the invading hoard under control. "My sister is determined to hook me up. The minute she sees you, she will devote the remainder of the morning to cute and embarrassing stories designed to impress you with my charm and delightfulness. Trust me, you'll want to stab knitting needles in your eyes after about ten minutes."

"Oh, I don't know, Logan." He had the temerity to smirk while crossing his arms over his chest. His broad, muscular chest. "I think I might enjoy the cute and embarrassing stories. And I already think you're charming and delightful."

My eyes widened in shock, and my mouth fell open yet again. "You do?"

"Logan? You digress." He snapped my pie hole

shut as he had before. But this time he didn't remove his hand. Instead, he stroked his forefinger lightly along my jaw, sending my pulse into a gallop to rival the Clydesdales pulling a beer wagon away from a crowd of alcoholic zombies.

"I do? Oh yeah. I do. So, anyway I thought if we gave her the impression we already had something going, well maybe it would divert her attention away from my relationship status for the day."

"I see," he murmured as he slipped his hand along the side of my neck and curled his fingers around my nape. Suddenly my knees buckled. I must have twisted my ankle more seriously than I thought. Fortunately, Morgan Kane caught me around the waist before I hit the ground and pulled me hard against him. I absently wondered if it would be considered rude to toss a breath mint in my mouth. Then it occurred to me I didn't have any. Oh well, moot point. His soft chuckle skittered along my skin like a physical caress. I swallowed hard. I tipped my head back, licked my lips enticingly, and closed my eyes, resigned and ready to make this sacrifice in an effort to thwart my sister and her underhanded plans. Kane chuckled again and then gently swept his lips over mine.

Except for Roger and that one tequila-induced-episode of poor judgment right after senior prom, I didn't have a whole lot of experience with men.

I know, I know. Up until now, I've sucked you into that whole sophisticated woman-about-town façade I wear so well, but really, it's true.

Morgan Kane, on the other hand, apparently knew his way around this town and most of the continental United States. The ground tilted, the sun spun backwards, and I had difficulty remembering my own name when Morgan Kane finally lifted his lips from mine. Would I never learn my impulsivity always comes back to bite me in the ass?

I coughed loudly, attempted to gather my wits, and looked around to gauge my sister's reaction. Denise, et al, was nowhere to be seen. The whole crew had apparently hustled past our lip-lock and continued into the house completely unnoticed. At least, by me. Kane's wicked grin said he was well aware of the effect he'd had on me, and it was precisely the one he'd intended. Wucking fonderful.

"Well, I could use a cup of coffee." He had the audacity to chuckle when I grabbed at his shirt to remain on my feet after he released me. Bad doggie. "How about you?"

Honestly, I was thinking I could use some ice water. About a gallon. Poured directly over my head.

"Coffee. Sure," I replied automatically while practically running along on my rubbery legs to keep up with his long strides. Denise waited at the back door, holding Clinique by the collar, and opening the door with a wide, knowing smile as we approached. And then my devious blonde sister and the Grim Reaper exchanged a wink. Well, damn! Had Yenta already been in cahoots with the Hellhound? Feaky snuckers!

Chapter 5

If I expected my family to be put out in any way by the sight of the Grim Reaper sitting at the kitchen table wolfing down bagels on a Sunday morning, I was doomed to disappointment. My family, the happiest group of crazies this side of the loony bin, sipped their coffee and made small talk just as though Death dropped by on a regular basis. I still had no idea what Kane was doing here, and the subject of developmental psychology had yet to be broached in the conversation swirling around my spinning head.

I gnawed morosely on my Long John, enjoying it less than usual, though realistically, nothing can truly destroy my love for doughnuts. Periodically I washed it, and my sense of disquiet, down my anxiety-constricted throat with a mouthful of double shot espresso. I wasn't upset over the fact my entire family knew the truth about my supernatural proclivities, not exactly. My nose was simply out of joint because no one had felt the need to let *me* in on the fact they knew. And I couldn't help wondering how many times my freakiness had been the topic of conversation unbeknownst to me. I *was* slightly perturbed, however, at my body's treacherous response to Morgan Kane's kiss. That hadn't been on my agenda for today or any other day. And the fact he'd directed neither a word nor a glance in my direction since we came in the house? Yeah, he was really on my last nerve.

Almost as though he'd read my mind, his glance suddenly swung in my direction.

"You have coconut on your chin," he remarked helpfully.

"I'm saving it for later."

"I see. Well, it's good to have goals." He pushed back his chair and turned to my father. "You wanna show me that '67 you've been bragging about all morning, Dan?"

My father, the car junkie, did not have to be asked twice. Brad followed them out, and as soon as the door banged closed behind the men, I grabbed a napkin from the basket in the center of the table and scrubbed furiously at my chin. Just as I suspected, clean as a whistle. I crumpled the napkin and dropped it on the table with a frown.

"You're mad at me, aren't you?" Denise stuck out her bottom lip and her chin trembled. With an eye-roll worthy of yours truly, my stepmother pushed back her chair and began clearing the table. Just as I got up to help her, the twins came tearing through the kitchen with a firmly leashed Clinique leading the charge.

The Petit Basset Griffon Vendéen didn't even pause to give me a friendly yip. Usually I was her favorite person in the whole wide world, and though I was a cat person who would never admit it, I felt a bit slighted when she shot past me as though I was yesterday's leftovers with all of the good bits picked over. A quick glance out the kitchen window confirmed she was galloping in the direction of the garage and the hot Hellhound. Traitor.

"Don't be ridiculous, Denise," I muttered. "Why

would I be mad at you? It's not your fault I was born some preternatural freak or that the Grim Reaper stopped by for coffee."

"Weeellll…" Denise drawled in a decidedly reluctant tone. "It sort of is. Oh, not the being born a preternatural freak, that's totally on you…but I did kind of invite Morgan for coffee."

"You what?" I spun on my sister so quickly I made myself dizzy. I grabbed the back of my chair to steady myself as she slumped down even further in hers. Big, fat tears welled up in her cornflower blue eyes and threatened to spill over onto her Passion Pink kissed cheeks. Well acquainted with my sister's ability to summon tears with the ease of a magician pulling a rabbit out of a hat, I wasn't buying the act. "And when exactly did you have a chance to invite Morgan Kane for coffee?"

"Thursday night?" she squeaked. Thursday night? But Denise and Brad had been at a medical society banquet Thursday night. I knew this because they'd asked me to babysit Mick and Vick.

"Sit down, Maxine," stepmother Gail sighed wearily. She pulled out my chair, and I sank into it, while she planted herself in the one across the table.

"When your father told us the truth about you and your, er…abilities, well it was a bit of a shock I can tell you," Gail began. "We were frightened to death, as you can imagine…"

"Of course you were," I croaked. My chest ached with impeding loss. I couldn't let them see how this hurt. My stepmother and I had grown so much closer over the last year. Now I would have to kiss that newfound sense of belonging good-bye. I'd never been like them. We all knew it. Now we simply had irrefutable proof. "All these years you've been cohabiting with a freak of nature. What better way to get rid of me than to fix me up with one of my own kind."

"Oh, Maxine, no…" Gail jumped from her chair, moved around the table, and pulled my face into her ample breasts. I couldn't speak. Partly because my throat was clogged with grief, and partly because I was certain I was a hairsbreadth away from suffocating.

Did I mention Gail has ample breasts?

Wooden chair legs scraped against the tile with the comforting squeal of a plastic fork on a Styrofoam plate. Oh, hell, Denise was going to hug me, too. I'd be sobbing like a reformed sinner at a revival meeting in a minute. I'm usually not much of a crier. I don't know why, but crying in front of people has never been me. Still, the combination of knowing I was an oddity in my own family coupled with the comforting arms of the only mother I'd ever known nearly did me in. A big fat tear hung on the edge of my lashes and threatened to actually course down my cheek. I bit my lip and prepared to disgrace myself. Imagine my surprise when instead of feeling my sister's reassuring arms around me, I felt the sharp sting of the three carat diamond eternity band Brad-the-Famous-Vascular-Surgeon had bestowed upon her on her last birthday as it connected with the back of my head.

"Ow!" I yelped, forgoing the comfort of Gail's cushy hooters to swivel my head and glare at my sister. "Mom, did you see what she did?"

"For the love of…Denise, don't smack your sister!" Gail cried in exasperation.

"Seriously Max, sometimes you are a complete dipwad. We weren't afraid *of* you. We were afraid *for* you." Denise crossed her arms over her chest, lowered her brows, and tried to appear intimidating. Well, as intimidating as a five foot six, willowy blonde perched upon stilettos and twinkling with bugle beads can manage. Yeah, I didn't find her especially threatening, either.

Being a firm believer in and frequent practitioner of gate control theory, I took a deep breath and chomped down on the inside of my cheek waiting for the pain messages originating in the back of my skull to be outwitted by the competing stimuli from my soon to be lacerated mouth. By the time I tasted the sweet metallic tang of blood, my head felt almost swell.

"If you were worried about what was involved, why did you go to Kane? Why not just ask me?"

"Dad said it was your decision whether or not to pursue the supernatural half of your nature," Denise replied glancing to her mother uncertainly. "He said it wasn't fair to let our fears influence you one way or the other."

"That's right. That's exactly what he said. He didn't say anything about asking Morgan, though," Gail smiled smugly.

Maybe not, but I was pretty sure he wouldn't have felt he needed to. In all of the years I'd known her, which was most of my life, I'd never known Gail to question my father. The fact she and Denise had sought out the Grim Reaper after Dad had all but expressly directed them to leave it alone? Well, I guessed it said something about their feelings for me.

"So you don't think I'm a freak?" I knew I was

grinning like an idiot, but I couldn't seem to help myself. They liked me. They really liked me.

"Of course you're a freak, Max." Denise patted my head as she scooted back to her seat. "But you're our freak, and we love you."

"Aw, that's so sweet, Denise," I drawled. "C'mon over here. I wanna give you a big hug. Around the neck. With a rope."

Gail chuckled. "Fight nice, girls. More coffee, Max?"

"Sure." I pushed my mug in her direction. It would take far more than a mind-bending kiss and some emotional upheaval to put me off my java.

"So what did Morgan have to say?" I injected as much nonchalance into my tone as I could muster. Judging by the knowing glance that passed between my sister and her mother, I wasn't entirely successful at hiding my interest.

"He assured us mistakes are very seldom made, so Retrievers aren't often in demand," Denise mumbled over her second bagel slathered with cream cheese. I loved my sister, but truth be known I resented the hell out of her metabolism. Just watching her eat made my ass expand. "He also said you're really, really good at it."

"Is that right?" I murmured absently. I didn't see any need to worry them further by sharing the number of supernatural snafus it had already been my pleasure to witness over the last year or so. On the other hand, my Retriever services had been called upon just once in all that time, so maybe there was some truth to what Kane had told them. "So if you already talked to him, what's he doing here now?"

"Your sister invited him," Gail said, plunking another mug of nirvana in front of me and resuming her seat. "She thinks he's hot."

"Yeah, well, it's probably just an unavoidable side effect of being born in the suburbs of Hell." I narrowed my eyes at my sister, who smirked and snagged a Long John from the blue platter in the middle of the table before she'd even finished licking the now devoured second bagel's cream cheese from her fingers. "By the way, I sincerely hope the next time you climb into your yoga pants, your ass resembles a nest of chipmunks fighting to get out of a trash bag."

Denise's tongue snaked out to catch a sticky gob of raspberry jam oozing from the Long John. She smacked her lips and grinned, well aware of my metabolism envy and entirely unimpressed by the threat of rodent butt.

"Well, judging by the lip lock you had going on out in the driveway, you don't exactly disagree with my assessment of Morgan Kane's appeal."

"That exhibition was entirely for your benefit, Denise. I was proactively attempting to thwart another of your thinly disguised schemes to hook me up."

"Uh huh."

"What's that supposed to mean?"

"It means I fully understand your need to rationalize your attraction to Morgan Kane. You are compelled to justify any hint of desire for another man due to your unacknowledged guilt." Denise nodded in her sage "I have three hundred and fifty-seven continuing education credits in psychology" manner.

"I don't have any unacknowledged guilt, Denise." I exploded. "Okay, I'll admit I blamed myself for my failure to retrieve Roger initially, but I understand now his death was part of some greater cosmic plan over which I had no control. It was not the result of my failed attempt to save him."

"While I'm thrilled to hear you have moved beyond your irrational belief you should have been able to save Roger when fate dictated otherwise, that isn't the guilt I was referring to."

"What choo talkin' 'bout, Denise?"

Yes, I had become defensive enough about the whole subject to revert to imitations of 1970s sitcom characters. If the quote fits, use it.

"I'm talking about your obvious inability to consider a relationship with a man without feeling as though you are being unfaithful to Roger." My sister sighed and casually flipped a curtain of butterscotch blonde hair over one dainty shoulder. I felt an uncharitable twinge of satisfaction when a few shiny strands caught in her bugle beads causing her to wince.

"Roger is dead, Denise. I don't have to be happy about it, but I have accepted it." Mostly. "Anyway, it's not technically possible to be unfaithful to a dead man, especially since we weren't even married at the time of his death."

"I know that, Max. I'm just not convinced you do. Finding someone new to love doesn't negate your feelings for Roger, you know. The guys I've introduced you to were nice, attractive, and successful, and you won't even give any one of them a chance."

"Well, duh, Denise."

See how easily I slip into witty comeback mode?

"Just because I cultivated no affection for any of the plaid-polyester-pantsed candidates you and Brad have paraded out for my inspection does not mean I am feeling guilty about anything. You do realize the compulsive wearing of polyester golf pants is just an advanced symptom of black cashmere socks disease, right?"

"For your information, Brad's socks today are navy blue and he hasn't removed the three pair of charcoal gray I slipped into his sock drawer last week." My sister raised her nose ever so slightly and sniffed.

"Sounds like you're making progress, Sis. Excellent!"

"All I'm saying is that Roger is dead and you aren't. It's not enough to just show up for your life, Max. You have to be willing to actually live it. Otherwise, what's the point?"

"The point is I *am* living my life. But honestly, Denise, while I won't rule out the possibility of finding love again, I just don't believe in fairytales anymore. If I'm out one night and lose my shoe when the clock strikes midnight, a rich, handsome prince is not going to knock on the door in the morning and slip it back on my fugly foot. I'll just be missing a shoe. By the way, have you checked Brad's slacks lately?"

"If you're out one night and lose your shoe, maybe you should worry less about fairytales and more about your tequila consumption."

Once she got in that snappy retort, my unsubtle reference to her husband's ongoing sock obsession and the potential for escalation into even more horrendous fashion choices that I'd thrown out there to distract her had the desired effect. My sister lapsed into silence as she switched from her psychological contemplation of my love life to the frightening implications of Brad's wardrobe. After all, navy blue and charcoal gray truly weren't very different from black. Maybe he was temporarily humoring her.

I gave my sister's guilt theory a moment of contemplation and then kicked it to the curb. Roger and I had a wonderful and loving marriage until the day we didn't. Despite the hurt and acrimony, we'd even managed to find our way back to one another because it was worth it. *We* were worth it. And when that awful moment came to say good-bye, we'd been given the chance. We'd been far luckier than many. Yes, I missed him. Yes, I was incredibly sad he wasn't here, but I'd found peace with it. Mostly. He would never begrudge me any happiness that might come my way; it just wasn't the stuff he was made of. Besides, Roger and I were in different places now, both literally and figuratively. It was a done deal, and I couldn't change it. My only alternative was to accept it, and I was sure I was doing okay with that. Denise was wrong. It wasn't guilt holding me back. It was fear. It was the fear I would never again find someone with whom I could be wholly myself, warts and all. Someone who would love me at my best and at my worst, both because of who I am, and in spite of it. I wasn't afraid of the plaid, polyester golf-pants.

Well, okay, maybe I was a little afraid of the plaid polyester golf-pants. I mean, they were barely one-step up on the evolutionary ladder from leisure suits and mullets in my book. And c'mon...they were polyester and plaid.

But mostly I was afraid I would never again find the degree of intimacy I'd had with Roger. No, I'm not talking about sex.

But you thought I was, didn't you?

Sex and intimacy aren't mutually exclusive. Let's face it. Sex without intimacy isn't just possible, it happens all the time. Don't get me wrong, I love the horizontal mambo as much as the next thirty-something girl in her sexual prime, but realistically? I wanted more. I wanted a man with whom I could feel comfortable enough to fart in bed without mortification. Not to say I would—I mean I do have some sense of propriety—but knowing I could. That is comfort. That is intimacy. That is a relationship, which having evolved beyond the giddy euphoria of first dates and new possibilities to the everyday mundane, is still as filled with love and passion as it was at the very beginning. I'd had that kind of comfort and intimacy once, and I wasn't sure how to find it again. It's not so easy to come by. I had to face facts. When you give someone the key to your heart, you also give them the key to your secrets. It's like handing them a free pass to hurt you because it gives them all the tools. Most days it seemed safer to be alone or settle for less, than to take the risk.

Chapter 6

Thankfully, the conversation switched gears to safer topics, as heavy footsteps thudded on the back steps, heralding the return of the men. Gail rose to add water to the coffee maker. The cartridge carousel, with every new and potentially appealing flavor on the market, was filled from the stash of boxes she and Denise compulsively collected and piled in a cabinet near the window.

A glance from beneath my lashes confirmed what I'd already suspected as Kane made his selection from those available. Morgan Kane was a purist. None of that French Vanilla Cinnamon Toast crap for him. Columbian Dark Roast. Straight up. My opinion of him climbed a notch. Anyone, supernatural or otherwise, who recognized the singular bliss of the unadulterated coffee bean was okay in my book.

"So what did you think of Daddy's third child?" I regarded Kane over the rim of my recently refilled mug.

"Sweet ride. Bet she gives him less headaches than his other two kids, too."

"Hey, now wait a minute," Denise piped up. "I can see why you'd say that about Max, but what the heck did I ever do to you?"

I suppose I should have been insulted and made some half-hearted effort to defend myself, but one does not argue with bald truth. Sometimes the best response is simply a smile and a one-fingered salute. I happily waved across the table at Denise while conveniently forgetting to use four of my fingers.

"Just saying," Denise mumbled, reaching for another bagel.

Have I mentioned the whole metabolism envy thing? Yeah, my sister was pushing that button especially hard, today.

"You drive her much, Logan?"

"Not anymore," my father interjected quickly. "Replacement parts for that baby are hard to come by, and Max can be somewhat, er, aggressive behind the wheel."

"That's not fair, Dad. I am not aggressive behind the wheel. I prefer to think of myself as the Queen of Strategic Vehicular Maneuvers."

"Well, plop a crown on your head and think of yourself any way you want, baby girl. It still took me six months to find a quarter panel the last time I let you get behind the wheel."

And people wonder where I get it.

A sound that might have been a chuckle, but I preferred to think was indigestion, rumbled up from Kane's chest as he brought his cup to his lips to hide a smile.

"Well, at least the car was salvageable, which is more than I can say for the sixty-nine muscle car you let Denise borrow for spring break."

My father's face fell, his shoulders drooped, and he shook his head with a sigh as he spared a fond thought for the candy-apple-red convertible that hadn't been good for anything other than tin cans and paper clips by the time Denise got home from Daytona Beach. Denise started to thumb her nose at me but quickly let her hand slip to the side, disguising it as an eye poke, as the twins came tearing through the door and bounded past us into the den with Clinique in hot pursuit.

"So, Denise, I understand you have quite the background in psychology." Kane cleared his throat and aimed a sly wink in my direction. "Are you familiar with the theory of psychosocial development?"

"Does a certain high profile billionaire need a new hairstyle?" Denise *pshawed* the notion there was any psychological theory with which she was not familiar with an airy wave of her hand. The one holding her bagel. Slathered in cream cheese and topped with strawberry jam. Her third, I believe, not that I was counting. Biotch.

"Well, then I guess I've come to the right place." Kane favored my sister with a heart stopping smile. At least it stopped my heart. "For the sake of argument, let's take a seventeen-year-old. Psychologically speaking, what can you tell me about behavior at that age?"

"Well..." Denise sat forward eagerly and licked her lips. Personally, I was wishing Brad-the-Famous-Vascular-Surgeon had substituted a stick of superglue for her lipstick this morning as I prepared to be bored into a coma. I yawned pointedly and reached for a Long John. Hell, if I was going to suffer through this mind-numbing diatribe, carbohydrate overload might make it slightly more palatable. "Unlike those who believe human psychological development was a series of psychosexual stages, Erikson theorized it was a series of stages impacted by social experiences. According to this theory, conflicts occur at every stage of development from birth until death. Successfully navigating these conflicts determines whether an individual develops ego strength or is left with a feeling of inadequacy. This sense of competence or failure motivates behaviors and actions."

"Fascinating." Kane tented his fingers on the table and leaned toward my sister as though the next words to fall from her lips might well be the answer to world peace. Seriously? Across the room, Brad-the-Famous-Vascular-Surgeon's lips twitched as he caught my eye and winked. Yeah, he'd heard it all before, too, but both of us would sit through it ten times rather than hurt Denise's feelings. She did have an impressive handle on this crap. Fortuitously—for him—Brad-the-Famous-Vascular-Surgeon's beeper chose that moment to go off. He reached for his belt and glanced down at the display, doing a lousy job of concealing his hopeful expression.

"Sorry, honey." He jumped from his chair and circled the table to drop a kiss on his wife's golden head. "There's a leaky aneurysm calling my name. I'll be home as soon as I can. Love you. 'Bye, everyone."

"Love you, too." My sister sighed at his retreating back and navy blue socks as he hurried out the door. "I wish someone would teach all those aneurysms, endarterectomies, and thrombectomies how to call someone else's name once in a while."

"People want the best," I reminded her. "If it was Mom or Dad, or me, or one of the girls…would you want some poor schmuck whose name cannot be recalled by a single aneurysm, endarterectomy, or thrombectomy doing the surgery, or would you want Brad?"

"Point taken. Besides, he promised to take two whole weeks off next month so we could spend some uninterrupted quality time together. I think he's ready for some downtime, too. Now where was I?"

Dad and Gail took advantage of Brad's sudden departure to jump to their feet and escape to the den on the pretext of checking on the twins who had been suspiciously quiet since coming in from the yard. Obviously, someone needed to see what the terrible twosome was up to in there. I observed my folks' clever defection with a fierce frown, sorry I hadn't thought up the excuse quickly enough to beat them to it. Denise smiled as though reading my mind and turned her attention back to the Grim Reaper.

"You were explaining how a person's sense of competence or failure in the mastery of psychosocial stages motivates behaviors and actions," Kane reminded her without skipping a beat. Was he kidding? I narrowed my eyes in his direction, wondering what he was up to.

Yes, he still sizzled, in case you were wondering, even through my day-old mascara-caked slits.

Was he actually paying attention to this psychodrivel? Kane struck me as a reasonably intelligent guy. He could have gone to the library. He could have surfed the Internet. He could have consulted a licensed therapist. After all, in his line of work he had to at least know someone who knew someone, right? A sudden epiphany struck, a sneaking suspicion he already knew the psychosocial development theory inside and out, and eliciting this explanation from my sister in my presence was entirely for my benefit. What I couldn't figure out was why. It wasn't anything *I* needed to hear.

I mean, c'mon, look at me. I've obviously mastered all of my psychosocial conflicts to date. I'm competent and confident and harbor no underlying fears of inadequacy. Well, except for that whole slightly over the hill, barren and childless, I need to lose ten pounds, what am I gonna do with the rest of my life thing I've got going on. Um, yeah. I sat up straighter and chomped off a mouthful of my doughnut, reveling in the sweet burst of raspberry exploding on my tongue as I struggled to pay attention. Sure, I was well adjusted, and I wasn't sure I even believed all the psychobabble my sister was so fond of spouting, but I probably shouldn't discount any opportunity for personal growth, right?

"Right!" Denise continued, happily. "So basically, in each stage of a person's life there is a specific conflict, a specific challenge if you will, and how an individual negotiates and resolves that challenge impacts psychosocial development. For instance, babies must resolve the conflict of trust versus mistrust. Because infants are entirely dependent. Whether or not their needs are consistently met will determine whether or not they develop trust or end up fearing the world is inconsistent and unpredictable. Does that make sense?"

"So the bottom line of this particular theory is that at any stage, a successfully navigated conflict results in ego strength and an unsuccessful resolution results in a sense of inadequacy?"

"Bingo! My work here is done." Denise clapped her hands together and stretched her arm across the table for another doughnut. Having surpassed the limit of what I could tolerate regarding her complete immunity to empty calories, I grabbed the edge of the platter and tugged it toward me and out of her reach.

"And the conflict for a teenager?" Kane left the question dangling in the air like a loaded pistol and turned his piercing green gaze in my direction. Seriously? Was the Grim Reaper implying I had failed to negotiate my own adolescent conflict successfully? My sense of self was just fine, thanks. Any confusion or insecurity I struggled with for now was a direct result of the fickle finger of fate poking me in the eye well after the age of thirty.

"Identity versus confusion," Denise supplied. "During adolescence, kids are taking those first tentative steps toward independence, seeking a sense of self. With the right encouragement and reinforcement, successful resolution in this stage results in a strong sense of self and a feeling of independence and control. Conversely, failure results in insecurity and confusion about the future."

"Fascinating."

"You already said that," I muttered, uncomfortably aware that though Kane directed his response to Denise, he continued to regard me intently, as though we were the only two people in the room. Denise seemed to realize, after having shared her expertise she effectively was being dismissed. Pushing her chair back from the table, she grabbed her mug and announced she'd better see what the kids were up to. She attempted to snag a doughnut as she passed me.

"You are tempting fate. And pissing me off. I have two words for you, Denise—Rodent Butt. Have mercy on your yoga pants and step away from the baked goods."

"You know, Max, sometimes you are just weird."

"And this is supposed to be a newsflash?"

"Yeah, I guess not," she laughed and headed toward the den leaving me alone with the doughnuts, the Grim Reaper, and an overactive sense of foreboding.

"Soooo..." I dropped my gaze and proceeded to draw amazing and intricate patterns in the loose coconut that had scattered on the tabletop during the consumption of my uber delicious Long John. I pushed a couple of stray strands back and forth with my finger before giving into temptation and popping them in my mouth, then asked, "What was that all about, exactly?"

"Maybe I was just making conversation." Kane shrugged. Really, this apparent obsession of his with drawing attention to the breadth of his shoulders was becoming tiresome. It was working, but it was tiresome.

"Maybe. And maybe I can leap tall buildings in a single bound."

"Logan, you aren't tall enough to leap an ottoman in a single bound." Kane's lips tilted up in a smile. I admit I was momentarily distracted. I was not, however, rendered speechless.

You may have correctly presumed by this time I seldom am.

I tilted my head back and looked down my nose with what I hoped was an expression of disdain.

"I rest my case."

His smile grew wider. My nerves stretched thinner. He was up to something, I just knew it.

"Were you paying attention to Denise's dissertation?"

"I've heard it so many times I could repeat it back verbatim. I would be happy to demonstrate. However there are no guarantees I will remain conscious until the end so maybe you could just cut to the chase?"

The Grim Reaper leaned back in his chair and stretched his long legs out in front of him.

"Tell me, what's your theory about identity versus confusion? Would you agree a teenager struggling to find himself and mostly failing would be prone to insecurity and confusion about right and wrong?" His bright green eyes bored into me, and I suppressed the urge to squirm like a naughty child being called on the carpet for her mischief.

"Are you implying I failed to resolve my adolescent conflict? Because I didn't, you know." Granted, insecurity rears its ugly head now and again, but I know right from wrong. Most of the time.

"I know this will come as a shock, Logan, but sometimes it isn't about you."

"I know that," I sniffed. "And in that case, yes, I agree. So who are we talking about?"

"Buddy."

Buddy, the thorn in my side, the stick in my spokes, the living breathing incompetent bumbler responsible for my untimely demise, broken bond, and currently questionable status as a supernatural superhero. *That* Buddy? Since Morgan Kane and I had only one slick-faced teen with a slippery façade of moderate acne, purple braces, and coke bottle thick glasses named Buddy in common, I assumed the worst. I reached for another Long John and shoved it in my pie hole. I had a hunch I would need all of the fortification I could get for whatever was coming, and besides it was chilly outside, and it's a known fact skinny girls freeze to death faster.

Chapter 7

"You have got to be kidding." I mumbled around a mouthful of raspberry stuffed pastry, favoring the Grim Reaper with an appalled expression. I swallowed my doughnut hard and washed it down with a rapidly cooling mouthful of coffee. "You honestly expect me to go into the Between and save that sorry weasel?"

"You did just agree with me that a teenager struggling to find himself and mostly failing would be prone to insecurity and confusion," Kane replied easily, utterly unmoved by the murderous look I was shooting across the table. "Sure the kid is a screw up, but maybe he just needs the right mentor to help him find his way."

"In that case, why don't *you* hoof it on over to the Between and get him yourself? Anyway, he's got uncles…why can't they take some responsibility for the kid?"

Buddy's uncles were estranged twins Marvin and Melvin Jenks. The former was the Director of the Office of Central Processing, the foul smelling outpost where I'd landing following my untimely demise. The latter was the fully licensed and bonded afterlife tour guide who served as Director of the Crossroads Visitor and Information Center who'd directed me to Dirk Kramer and Roger on my introductory soul retrieval mission. Both were small, nervous men with a penchant for poorly tailored suits and wire rimmed glasses, and both were laboring under the delusion they were fooling people into believing they had a lush head of hair with their oh-so-sexy comb-overs.

"Look, I wouldn't ask but, though I can cross over, unlike you I can't bring anyone back with me." Kane shook his head ruefully. "And as you're well aware, his uncles didn't have a whole lot of luck with the kid. I was thinking maybe he would benefit from a woman's touch," Kane continued in that maddeningly conversational tone.

"Has anyone ever told you you're about as subtle as a two by four to the back of the head?" I replied slowly, sucking the coconut crumbs from my fingers and noting with interest how Kane's eyes were glued to my mouth. He grinned, and I was struck yet again by the sheer perfection of his features sans scars. This could not be good.

"Once or twice."

"I know you can't be suggesting *I* babysit him since we both know I would rather douse myself in lighter fluid and run naked through Hell than have anything whatsoever to do with Buddy the Bungler."

"Actually, Logan, you were exactly who I had in mind."

"C'mon, Kane. He killed me, for the love of Pete! And he killed Roger, too." I didn't owe the little weasel anything except maybe a nice big pat on the back while he was standing on the edge of a cliff.

"Severing your soul was an accident, Logan. He was just trying to be a big shot and make an impression. Please refer to Denise's lecture and the consequences of an unresolved psychosocial conflict. As for Roger,

Buddy may have taken down the plane, but I'm the one who severed Roger's soul and only because it was his time. If it hadn't been the plane crash it would have been something else, so if you're looking for someone to blame, look no further. That's on me."

I knew he'd been the one to sever Roger's soul. Kane and I had discussed it shortly after Roger's death, and I'd decided if Roger had to go, I'd rather it was Morgan Kane who'd been assigned to take him out than some strange, uncaring Grim Reaper. At least Kane was compassionate. Or so I'd believed until he suggested I take on Buddy the Bungler as my own personal pet project. He wasn't compassionate; he was crazy. What did I know about straightening out a screwed-up teenager? I had enough trouble straightening myself out. Did this man not know me at all?

"You know I don't hold you responsible for Roger's death, Morgan." The Grim Reaper's gaze slid to the side and his Adam's apple bobbed as he nodded shortly. I realized then that maybe he *had* thought I blamed him. Of course, I hadn't been taking his calls, and there was that ugly scene after I returned from the Between without Roger. I'd never been intended to retrieve him in the first place, and everyone in the supernatural hierarchy apparently knew it in advance, except me. To say I had not taken the news well might be a teeny understatement. A major meltdown, copious tears, and an attempted throttling of the Grim Reaper by yours truly had been involved. So okay, maybe I could see how he might think I blamed him just a bit. My bad.

"Seriously, even if I didn't detest the little shit, I hardly think I'm the best role model. I mean, let's face it, I could screw up a one car funeral. Find somebody else."

The chair legs scraped loudly against the floor tile as he pushed back his chair and rose to his full, intimidating height. He forked a hand through his hair, obviously forgetting he'd tied it back. With half of it falling around his newly perfect face, he tugged out the elastic band and shook it all free in the manner of an aggravated lion, and then gathered it back into a slick new ponytail.

"There isn't anyone else. Alicia is busy with the baby and I may be...indisposed for a while. And maybe someone who could screw up a one car funeral is exactly what he needs. Maybe he can relate to you." Alicia was the official Superintendent of Spiritual Impediment, aka SSI, who—when the mood struck her—could glow like a radioactive Christmas tree. On steroids. She also had a toddler named Esmeralda who had inherited the talent and who, I assumed, would one day step into her mother's perpetually radiant kitten heels. I only hoped the child had also inherited her mother's beautifully pedicured feet and taste in footwear.

"Indisposed?"

"I'll be distracting my cousin while you get Buddy out."

"Cerberus? Oh my stars, Kane! I gave you far more credit. You don't mean to tell me you're going to deliberately seek out that smoking pile of chrome and leather? You said it yourself, he wants you back on his team, and he nearly tore you to ribbons the last time you crossed his path."

"Because he shifted and I didn't. Otherwise, we're pretty evenly matched. Won't make that mistake again.

And no, I don't trust the mangy mutt as far as I can throw him, but Buddy's just a kid, Logan. Don't you think he deserves a second chance?"

Did I think he deserved a second chance? Seems it wasn't all that long ago I was waxing poetic about second chances. I'd been given a lot of them. A second chance at life, a second chance with Roger, a second chance to be a welcome and productive member of my family. For a while I'd become my own worst enemy, and I'd been a lot older than Buddy when I tumbled into that trap. I couldn't help remembering one of the last times I'd seen him. It was while I was on the other side, in the Between, still believing I could save Roger. Buddy was running through the middle of a field, and the Seekers, Cerberus' diaphanous black shadows that look like big creepy worms, surrounded him in a funnel cloud. His eyes wild, he mouthed the words *help me* before they consumed him completely, and both Buddy and the Seekers disappeared. Apparently, he'd realized by then that trying his luck on the dark side hadn't resulted in the jackpot payoff he'd been hoping for. Having enough of my own problems to worry about at the time, I'd attributed the unsettling twinge of sympathy and concern I felt for the incompetent nincompoop to indigestion, as a result of the cookies and lemonade I'd consumed at the Timekeeper's cottage before setting out on my retrieval mission. Citrus and I are not friends. Honestly, I hadn't really given Buddy much thought over the last year. I hated to admit it, but Kane was right. Buddy was just a kid. And he deserved a second chance. Probably.

Hell, if it's not one thing it's another, and in my case, it's often the same thing twice. I pushed back my chair and climbed slowly to my feet while exhaling a loud, dramatic sigh designed to wordlessly communicate my opinion of the entire situation.

"What do I have to do?"

Morgan Kane, Hellhound, aka the Grim Reaper, froze for a moment as though unsure he'd heard me correctly, and then he favored me with a blinding smile that caused my heart to stutter like the alternator on my old jalopy.

"Personally, I think my cousin realizes he bit off more than he could chew and will be glad to get the kid out of his hair. Of course, that doesn't mean he'll admit it and give him up without a fight. You get him out, and when I get back, I'll take him off your hands. Just try to have some patience with him for however long it takes, huh?"

I wondered if Kane actually believed any of this was going to go smoothly. Even if Cerberus felt unusually agreeable, which in my opinion was about as likely as my winning a gardening competition, there was still the wildcard named Buddy to consider.

"I'll do my best, Kane. But you should know while patience may be a virtue, sometimes I think it's a lot more effective to just slap the stupid out of someone."

"Somehow, Logan, I figured as much. Just try not to kill him until I get back, okay?"

"What? Oh, yeah, restraint, sure thing." He was smiling again, and I was slightly vexed to discover I was having a real problem concentrating on what he was saying. Frankly, I didn't understand my reaction. I mean okay, so I'd always thought he was a hot commodity even with the scars, and now that they had magically all but disappeared, he was—well, he was just my flavor of handsome. But I'd never had any difficulty with conversation in his presence before. Well, except for that embarrassing moment I found myself naked in his cabin and discovered he'd laundered my panties.

Can we say awkward, boys and girls?

Then again, he'd never kissed me into a lump of putty before, either.

"What happened to your scars?" I asked suddenly.

Yes, I can always be counted on for my subtlety. I did warn you.

"Hellhounds heal fairly quickly if they stay in their animal form," he replied with a lift of his shoulders. His broad, muscular shoulders. "I've been shifting as often as I can."

"Uh huh."

I narrowed my eyes and tried to picture him in plaid, polyester golf-pants hoping the visual would put to rest the odd flutter in my nether regions. It might have worked if it hadn't occurred to me polyester would cling like a second skin to his firm and magnificent buttocks. As appealing as that thought was, I admitted to myself there was more to recommend Morgan Kane than an exceptional posterior. I remembered the dogwood and gin he'd left in my kitchen the night before Roger's funeral. It had been incredibly thoughtful. It was a lovely reminder that gave me hope at a time I had very little left to keep me breathing. Somehow, he'd known it was exactly what I needed. The dogwood, that is. The gin gave me a hangover the size of Texas.

"Logan?"

"Huh? What?" I snapped back to reality. The tone

of his voice and the puzzled expression told me he'd had to repeat himself more than once to get my attention.

"Why are you squinting at me like a miner's mule on his first expedition into the sunlight?" Stepping closer, he cupped my chin and tipped my head back.

"Though I'm rendered nearly speechless by that lovely compliment, I do have a question. Reaper," I croaked as he leaned in so close that his warm breath fanned my face. I decided that was the reason my cheeks suddenly felt so heated.

Yep, I was going with that.

"How do you feel about polyester?"

He arched a brow over one sparkling, emerald eye. "Polyester and I are not friends. More of a flannel and denim guy, myself."

"Okay," I breathed. "How about golf?"

"Beautiful walk ruined by a little white ball."

Lordy, except for the whole scythe-wielding severer of souls thing, Morgan Kane was turning out to be darn near perfect. Taking a deep breath and gripping the back of the chair in preparation for the crushing disappointment I knew was inevitable, I cleared my throat and asked the all-important question.

"What color are your socks?"

He burst out laughing, and I felt something shift in the region of my heart. I'd never really heard him laugh before. I suppose that shouldn't be surprising considering our rather unorthodox meeting and relationship to date. Not to mention his line of work.

To recap: After being forced to re-evaluate everything I'd ever believed about myself and my family, I'd ventured out into a freakin' blizzard with a sadistic voice in a box who played navigator. I nearly died of exposure, was rescued by a large black Hellhound I thought was going to eat me (and not in a good way), who then turned out to be the Grim Reaper. As if that wasn't enough adventure for one day, after peeing my pants, I was forced to drink *tea*, and hoofed my butt on over to the afterlife. I rescued a man I mostly despise and was forced to say good-bye to the man I loved. With the helpful assistance of a large white Hellhound who pushed me into a lake—aka portal between dimensions opened courtesy of my mom's necklace—I crashed back into the land of the living like a bag of wet cement on a very hard floor—it hurt like hell—and I tried to strangle the Grim Reaper. Not your typical InternetCupid.com introduction, right?

Maybe I should consider taking my act on the road.
"Excuse me?"
"Your socks…what color are your socks?"
"How is that relevant?"
"They aren't black cashmere, are they?"
"Are you off your medication again, Logan?" He shook his head with a grin and twitched up the hem of his jeans to expose an ankle clad in a diamond pattern of yellow and blue. The argyles didn't even come close to matching a single thing he was wearing. "Happy?"

Yep. A little too happy for my own piece of mind, if you want to know the truth.

Standing in my father's kitchen with my entire family in the next room, I found myself considering Morgan Kane with the exact same heart thumping, sweaty palmed, tummy twisting eagerness I usually reserved for a second piece of chocolate lava cake with hot fudge sauce and whipped cream. Real whipped cream, not that fake, non-dairy product that can double as modeling clay when it sits too long. The Grim Reaper was just as decadent, delicious, and dangerous as any dessert I'd ever craved. I knew the wise thing was to push the plate away and get up from the table, resisting the urge to scramble for a fork and dive right in. I knew indulgence might be a bad idea...a very, very bad idea. However, I think we have established I am inherently incapable of exhibiting any willpower whatsoever in the presence of tempting carbohydrates.

What? You thought my cellulite magically appeared all by itself?

I reached up and grabbed him by the hair and pulled his lips to mine. One little taste couldn't hurt, right?

Chapter 8

Apparently, it could. As the breath left my lungs and my bones dissolved, I heard a panicked voice in some far distant corner of my mind hinting that maybe one little taste wasn't enough. When Roger had been alive, I'd enjoyed frequent, generous servings of chocolate lava cake with hot fudge sauce and whipped cream. Over the last year, I'd eliminated it from my diet completely and thought I'd grown accustomed to bland, processed snack food. Clearly, abstinence did not make chocolate lava cake with hot fudge sauce and whipped cream any less appealing. In fact, in some strange fashion, it made it taste even better.

"What was that for?" Kane murmured against my lips as I unclenched my fists from his hair.

"I thought I heard Denise coming," I covered brilliantly.

"Ah," he whispered before claiming my lips again for a second helping.

"What was that for?" I gasped as he pulled away and straightened to his full height.

"Just in case."

"In case of what?"

"I'll pick you up later. We'll use the portal at my place again."

It didn't escape my notice he'd avoided my question, but I attributed his skillful evasion to the sound of footsteps in the hallway. My family had returned. I fleetingly wondered if I could use the *Denise is coming* excuse to grab another bite of chocolate lava cake, but Kane stepped away. "After we go through the portal, I want you to concentrate on getting Buddy and getting out. No matter what happens, Logan, just grab the kid and get yourself out."

I didn't care for the sound of that at all. In fact, I heard echoes of his instructions to me the last time I'd ventured across dimensions and couldn't help remembering I hadn't been given the whole story. Perhaps the Grim Reaper shared my misgivings about this entire mission not being quite as cut and dried as he tried to make it appear. He shrugged.

And yes, I noticed the breadth of his shoulders, yet again. I'm not blind, people.

"Keep an eye on him, maybe pretend he's your younger brother."

"I would have smacked the crap out of the little shit long ago if he was my brother."

"Point taken." Kane's teeth flashed briefly. "Okay, then pretend he's a good friend's younger, and very annoying, brother. Give him some responsibility. Make him toe the line and try not to kill him until I get back. Think you can manage that?"

I didn't think anything of the sort, but I figured since he was on his way to commune with Cerberus, the least I could do was give him one less thing to worry about.

See how thoughtful and selfless I've become?

"No problem."

"Great. Gotta run. See you around six." My family arrived back in the kitchen just as Kane reached for the door. "Dan, Gail, thanks for the coffee and the company. Denise, thanks for the education." He nodded at each of them in turn, then his gaze locked with mine, burning with an odd intensity. "See you later, Logan."

"Right," I whispered. And then he was gone, and along with him went any confidence I had in the whole cockamamie plan. I tried to believe his story that Cerberus would be happy to get rid of Buddy, and Kane's distracting him was just a formality, but my bullshit alarm was clanging loudly enough to give me a headache. There was more to this story. I knew it as surely as I knew that chocolate is a health food. Think about it. Chocolate is made from cocoa beans. Cocoa beans grow on a bush. A bush is a plant. A vegetable is a plant. Vegetables are good for you. Therefore, chocolate is a health food.

You're welcome. Hey, I said I could rationalize. I didn't say it always works. Seriously, I just gave you a perfectly good excuse for eating as much chocolate as you want, and you're going to criticize?

Something about this whole thing smelled just shy of rancid, and I was damn sure planning to find out what it was before Kane and I left for the Between.

"See you later, Logan?" my sister mimicked with a hopeful grin. "Dare I assume you have a date with the ass-tastick Grim Reaper?"

"I guess it depends on your definition of a date, Denise. Kane will be going over to the other side, as will I. He will be paying his cousin, Cerberus, a visit. I will be staying as far away from Cerberus as humanly or inhumanly possible. We will, however, be sharing a mutual goal which is to rescue Buddy, the incompetent Grim Reaper in Training who killed me last year. If that constitutes a date in your world, then yep, we've definitely got it going on."

"I can work with it." Denise flipped her butterscotch blond hair over one shoulder. "Now go hop in the shower and get dressed. It's already noon and we have a lot of shopping to do and not much time to do it."

"I'm already dressed, and I have no desire to go shopping."

Denise's perfectly manicured brows drew together in an inverted V as her gaze raked me from head to toe. "You weren't planning on wearing *that*, were you?"

"Of course not," I replied with a healthy dose of scorn. As if I would even consider wearing this uncoordinated and uniquely me ensemble to the other side. Well, at least I wouldn't now that my fashion forward younger sibling had given it the hairy eyeball. "But I wasn't planning on going shopping either. I was planning on doing laundry."

"Oh yeah, as if that's gonna happen before the second Tuesday of next week." Denise rolled her eyes and both my father and step-mother bit back a laugh. Gail wasn't quite successful at hiding her amusement, but to give him props, Dad did manage to convert his guffaw into a slightly believable cough. My love of laundry was legendary in my family.

"Denise, you know I detest shopping." I sighed. It wasn't the actual shopping I hated so much as that moment of inevitable disappointment.

Oh, please! You know exactly what I mean.

…That moment you spot the most brilliant, perfect, awesome, sexy ensemble and rush into the fitting room with hangers draped over your arm, prepared to rock the world. You wriggle into said brilliant, perfect, awesome, sexy ensemble while clinging to your inaccurate illusion of your actual height, weight, and body type. Trapped inside the cubicle you push, pull, and contort yourself into physically impossible positions in an attempt to tame the jiggly bits defying you at every turn. At last, you turn to face the mirror expecting a runway model, and then you're forced to wonder when the hell the short, round troll wearing your brilliant, perfect, awesome, sexy ensemble sneaked into the dressing room and hopped in front of you. Shopping was not worth the ego smack.

"Shopping is an acquired skill, sister mine. You simply have not yet learned to select items that work for you. What you need is a personal fashion advisor. Because I love you, I am willing to assume the burden. You may thank me later. Time's a wasting, so forget the shower for now, just go run a comb through that rat's nest currently masquerading as your hair, grab your purse, and let's go. Mom and Dad will keep an eye on the girls for a while, right?"

"Anyway," I stalled while rinsing out the used coffee mugs and stacking them in the dishwasher, green on the left, blue on the right, just the way Gail preferred them. "I don't get paid until next week, so I really can't afford to go shopping."

"Max," my sister said quietly, coming up behind me, wrapping her arms around my shoulders, and giving me a gentle squeeze. "Roger left you more money than you'll ever spend. He's been gone for over a year, and you haven't touched a penny of it. Not to mention the tidy sum you got for the condo. What's holding you back? Roger couldn't take it with him, and you can't either. He would want you to enjoy that money. You know he would."

What *was* holding me back? Was it simply that I'd learned to embrace Lifestyles of the Necessarily Frugal, or was it that it still didn't feel as though the money was mine? Which was ridiculous. I was fairly certain the U.S. Treasury Department didn't print a single bill that would be accepted as legal tender in the Between, the Crossroads, the Office of Central Processing, or whatever other little enclave of the afterlife Roger was now calling home. I looked down at my sadly rumpled attire. If I was honest with myself, it wasn't that different from the rest of my wardrobe currently biding its time in the laundry basket, hoping to get lucky. So maybe I should use some of *my* money and go shopping?

"Well, if I do decide to take my life in my hands and agree to let you take me shopping, you have to promise me we'll be back by four," I offered in a cautious tone. Knowing Denise, I harbored a reasonable fear we could disappear into retail hell for days. "I have to get in the shower, and you know how long it takes for my hair to dry."

The enthusiasm with which my sister Denise acknowledged my reluctant agreement to accompany her on a retail expedition cannot be overstated. You may think you've seen the epitome of excitement on one of those television commercials where they show up unannounced at some poor sap's door with balloons and a giant check for an obscene amount of cash. Those people have nothing on my sister. After squeezing the life out of me and dancing an ungainly jig around the kitchen, barely able to believe her good fortune, Denise sat down at the kitchen table with a pen and paper and commenced the development of a complicated and strategic attack on the mall that would have put the Joint Chiefs to shame. I guess everyone has to be good at something. I shot a nervous glance in Gail's direction. No help there. She squeezed some lemon-scented liquid detergent into the dishwasher, closed the door, and hit the wash cycle before returning my look with an expression that clearly told me she believed I'd lost my mind. Oh well, I was up to my neck in it now and maybe I'd get lucky and find something in my size. Something that was neither pink, pea soup green, nor constructed of fleece. Hey, even the wicked witch was just trying to get her hands on a good pair of shoes.

Chapter 9

In my defense, I'd actually fallen for the charade that we were going shopping for *me*. Two hours, eight shopping bags, and three shoeboxes later, my head throbbed, my feet ached, and I'd yet to purchase a single item. Denise, on the other hand, had managed to acquire half of her new spring wardrobe. I wasn't trying to be difficult, I swear. It's just that Denise and I had wildly divergent opinions on appropriate wardrobe choices for a foray into the afterlife. Acutely aware I would be spending at least a period of time with Morgan Kane, Denise was advocating high class hooker-wear, while I was stubbornly clinging to the practicality of cargo pants and combat boots. It appeared I was destined to return to my one bedroom over garage empty handed and sadly fated to renew my relationship with my stackable washing machine. And then it happened.

As I schlepped along in Denise's wake, half-heartedly stepping on the backs of her shoes, too tired and frustrated to be more than mildly amused at the way it caused her to wobble in an attempt to regain her balance, it was as though a celestial spotlight suddenly shone from above. I won't swear to it, but it's entirely possible I also heard angels sing. I stopped, released the bags from my cramped fingers, and simply stared. There in the window of Lucky Larry's Luscious

Leather Goods, displayed seductively between an interesting selection of metal studded collars and something suspiciously resembling an item of lingerie constructed of straps and chains, was my idea of the perfect afterworld attire. Hallelujah! It was a Christmas miracle in March right in the middle of the Tannerstown Outlet Mall.

I moved toward the entrance with the single-mindedness of a mid-western cow caught in an alien's tractor beam, oblivious to my sister who was high-tailing it back in my direction while screaming dire warnings of doom.

"No, Max, no. Step away from the leather. Step away from the leather! Honey, you haven't got the ass for it."

Skidding to a stop, shopping bags scattered around her, Denise groped wildly for my arm, but it was too late. I had crossed the threshold and Lucky Larry himself, rubbing his nicotine stained palms together, and wearing an oily smile, moved out from behind the counter to attend to my needs. Undeterred by the crinkling of paper behind me as Denise retrieved her bags, immune to her mumbled monologue lamenting the complete impropriety of leather pants on anyone over the age of eighteen, I slowly raised my arm and pointed reverently to the window display.

"Size?" Lucky Larry leered, flicking his tongue over his thin lips and running his gaze over me from head to toe. Both the question and the leer gave me pause. For one thing, I had no desire to share the size of my ass with Lucky Larry. For another, I was willing to bet that despite the title he wore so proudly, with his stringy hair, pigeon chest, and dirty fingernails, Larry hadn't gotten lucky in a long, long time. I hated to break it to him, but even if he offered me fifty percent off, his losing streak wasn't about to change.

"Uh, I'm not sure…just give me one of each and I'll decide which fits the best." I hedged as he shuffled toward the display.

"Color?"

"Black, naturally."

"Well, at least I've managed to teach you something," Denise huffed up behind me and collapsed onto a bench outside the curtain-covered doorway of the fitting room. I'm sure my sister assumed I'd chosen black due to its universally recognized slimming qualities. While I was all over that idea, she was probably giving me too much credit. Loathe to disabuse her of the notion there might, indeed, be hope for her persistently style-challenged older sibling, I simply smiled and nodded agreeably. Actually, the choice had far less to do with her fashion tutelage than with previous experience. Roger's Aran sweater, jeans, and tennis shoes hadn't served me very well on my previous expedition to the other side.

Need I elaborate on the discomfort of wet, dirty wool with insulating properties?

I'd decided if I ever suffered an attack of temporary insanity and agreed to return to the afterlife, I would definitely dress appropriately. Leather seemed the logical choice for creeping fog, swirling dust, and sudden unpredictable downpours. Besides, if I was going to be a supernatural superhero, I should at least look the part, right? Let's face it, black leather and boots are way more kick-ass than jeans and tennis shoes no matter what dimension one finds oneself in.

Gathering an armload of tanned and dyed cowhide, I dumped the pile into Denise's lap and stepped into the dressing room, tugging the curtain into place. As she handed them in to me, I attempted to squeeze into one pair after another.

"Much too big," I announced, tossing the first pair aside and reaching through the curtain for another which Denise obligingly slapped into my palm. After numerous contortions, the outcome was clear.

"Way too small," I gasped, sticking my arm through the curtain.

"Who are you? Goldilocks?' Denise muttered from outside the cubicle.

"Apparently I am," I crowed, yanking the curtain aside triumphantly. "Because this pair is just right!" Well, assuming I was willing to ignore the twelve inches of leather trailing beyond my feet. Otherwise, the fit was more awesome than I could have ever hoped. Soft as butter, the leathers clung to my thighs like a second skin, squeezed and lifted my butt, and cinched in my waist at just the right spot. I twirled in the mirror, admiring myself from every angle. I was in love. Now all I needed was a good pair of stilts.

I stepped out of the fitting room and was gratified to see my sister's professionally arched brows take a one-way trip to her hairline.

"I have to admit, I had my doubts, but except for the length, those do look pretty awesome on you, Max," she grinned. "You should definitely get them."

"Ya think?" I regarded myself doubtfully. "I won't be able to wear them tonight, though. I doubt there's a pair of heels on the market that can make up the difference, even assuming I'd be able to walk in them.

These need to be shortened at least a foot."

"Nikos can have them ready by five if we get there within the next hour or so."

"Seriously?"

Things were looking up. I peeled the awesomeness that was my soon to be new leather pants from my butt and poked my legs back into my jeans. While I dressed, Denise managed to pile two additional pairs of pants on the counter, along with some kick-ass boots sporting a sensually curved, but manageable one-inch heel, a bright blue T-shirt, and a black leather jacket that looked like it should come with its own motorcycle. Apparently, when my sister decides to get on board, she prefers a yacht to a rowboat.

Shaking my head, I dug in my purse for my credit card and then stood by patiently while Lucky Larry rang up my purchases. He hit the final key and I wondered if that jacket really did come with its own motorcycle. Perhaps I should have checked the price tags. The grand total exceeded what I earned in a month working at my dad's hardware store. The room began to swim, and I swayed on my feet. Denise simply plucked the plastic from my numb fingers and handed it over.

"Sign here." She pushed the receipt in front of me, sighed, and wrapped her fingers around mine, pushing the pen along the line until the dirty deed was done. Then she shoved the bags into my arms, picked up her own, and grabbed my sleeve, marching me out of the mall to her car.

"Feel better?" Denise asked once we'd loaded our purchases into her sparkling blue BMW X5 luxury SUV and buckled ourselves into our heated seats with lumbar support.

"I just dropped a month's salary because a pair of pants made my ass look great. Of course, I don't feel better!" I snapped.

"You can easily afford it, Max."

"No, I can't. My paycheck doesn't stretch…"

"Roger is gone, Max."

"Well, duh. No shit, Sherlock. What does that have to do with anything?"

"You've been scrimping by on what you make for the last year, exactly the way you did before he died. You refuse to touch the damn money."

"I certainly do not." I lifted my nose in the air with a sniff of superiority. "I take money out every month."

"How much?" Denise demanded.

"What?"

"How much? How much do you take out every month?"

"Twelve hundred dollars," I announced haughtily. I didn't even understand why we were having this conversation. Denise and Brad had more money than God. Why was she suddenly so concerned about *my* financial affairs?

"Okay, so let's see." She tapped a petal pink nail on the steering wheel as though she was deep in thought. "Twelve hundred dollars a month is probably less than the interest the account generates but coincidentally, it's the exact amount you received in alimony. So every month, a check arrives in the mail from Roger's bank in the exact amount of your alimony, just as it did every month when Roger was still alive."

"Shut up, Denise." I didn't like where this conversation was going. Every time my sister assumed that particular tone of voice and began to point out things that should have been obvious to me, and weren't, she usually ended up being right.

Need I tell you how annoying that can be?

"You've created a bubble of make-believe where you can pretend nothing's changed. You can't bring yourself to access a penny over your regular alimony from that account because you feel guilty using it. It would be akin to acknowledging his absence wasn't temporary."

Had I been living in a bubble? Well, if I was, obviously it was working for me. So, big deal. I have a bubble. I like it in my bubble. It's my freakin' bubble.

"Why couldn't you just leave my bubble alone?" All I'd wanted was a pair of leather pants that made my ass look great. What I'd gotten was an enormous balance on my credit card and an unasked for intervention from my sister, the Psychology Queen. Well, and I actually *had* gotten leather pants that made my ass look great.

"Because I love you. I know you don't do change, Max. Hell, everyone on the planet knows it, but you deserve better than half a life. I just want you to take a chance, embrace life, be happy." Denise reached across the console and tentatively laid a hand on my thigh. After debating for a minute whether or not to simply cold-cock her, I gripped her fingers and squeezed. There's no map for navigating the pothole-rutted road of loss—no street signs, no compass, no helpful stranger standing on the corner to point you in the right direction. Ultimately, you drive through the dark alone, gripping the wheel with nothing except guts and fear, until one day you blink and realize you've arrived at the intersection of I-Will-Never-Forget-You Street and Life-Goes-On Avenue. Now it was time to take a hard right and proceed onto Taking-the-Next-Step Boulevard.

I wonder if they sell a GPS for that?

"I know he's gone, Denise. I was there. Remember? But while change and I have never been friends, I voluntarily kissed Morgan Kane, didn't I?"

"I thought that was strictly for my benefit?"

"Well, yeah…it was. The first time, anyway," I mumbled.

"The first time?" Denise squealed. "And it didn't make you feel guilty?"

"Of course it made me feel guilty."

"I knew it," she sighed. "You felt like you were being disloyal to Roger, right?"

"Um, not exactly." I hesitated. "Actually, I felt guilty that I didn't feel very guilty. Do you think that's normal?"

"Really? That's great." Denise clapped her hands like a small child.

"So I'm normal?"

"Well, I wouldn't go that far. But your reaction? Definitely normal. You, my dear sister, are ready to move on."

"Yeah, I guess maybe I am." I took a deep breath and blew it out. Then I offered my sister a smile. "But, promise me there will be no more plaid polyester. Anyway, you were right about one thing. It was comfortable there in my bubble. At least it was until you went and stuck your pointy nose in my bubble and popped it. You seriously are a pain in the ass, sometimes."

"I'm sorry," Denise sniffed. "It's just that if you have trouble seeing the forest for the trees, I figure it's my job to slam your head into a trunk now and then to wake you up if the occasion warrants. That's what sisters do."

"You do know how much I hate it when you're right, don't you?"

"It's hard to forget since you're always so happy to remind me."

"Hand over your phone."

"My phone? Why?"

"Because I left mine on the table at Dad's and I need to access my bank account. I'm going to increase my monthly allowance to fourteen hundred," I suddenly decided.

"Woo-hoo, a whole two hundred bucks. Don't spend it all in one place," Denise snarked as she dug in her purse before handing over the state-of-the-art device. Denise had an app for just about everything on the damn planet. She could remotely turn her house lights off and on, adjust the thermostats, lock the doors, and set the alarms at the touch of a button. The only thing she couldn't do via phone was the laundry. If they ever come out with an app for that, I am all over it. Seriously.

"Spendthrift is not my style. It's not the amount that's important anyway, it's the symbolism, right?"

"I guess so," she agreed, inserting the key in the ignition and cranking over the motor. "And just for the record? You don't have to prove anything to me, so I hope you aren't just sitting there playing with apps to make me shut up."

"I'm not doing it to prove anything to you. Maybe I

need to prove something to me."

I bit my lip and punched at the screen, feeling a burden lift that I hadn't even realized was weighing me down. Honestly, one would think I'd know myself better by now. Let's be clear, my insight is occasionally flawed. But this is the way it's supposed to be, right? I mean, I *am* a self-proclaimed expert on Kubler-Ross, after all. Denial, anger, bargaining, depression, and acceptance. Kubler-Ross said the order of the stages may differ by individual, and not every person may experience every stage. I'd kind of skipped over denial and bargaining. I mean, I was there and everything seemed pretty black and white, so both seemed rather pointless. Anger and depression? Uh, check. But, I'd done it. I'd reached acceptance. So now what? Now I was going to cherish the past, be slightly less frugal, wear leather pants that made my ass look great, and acknowledge I was possibly, maybe, sort of attracted to the Grim Reaper.

"There." I handed the phone back to Denise. "And for the record? Let's face it, Denise. There isn't an app on the planet that's capable of shutting you up."

Chapter 10

"Holy Hell's Angels," my father exclaimed when I'd donned my newly tailored ass-enhancing leather pants along with the T-shirt, boots, and jacket Denise had chosen and wandered into his kitchen to await the arrival of the Grim Reaper. Not exactly the reaction I was going for, but I suppose it would have been kind of creepy if Dad had remarked instead on my shapely butt. My mother's fugly necklace, a heavy and ornate baroque-styled pendant with a huge cabochon in the center ringed by smaller facet-cut stones was currently zipped securely in the inside pocket of my jacket, easily accessible but unable to spoil the perfection of my nifty new ensemble. Aside from the sentimental value, it could hardly be considered a fashionable accessory and was really a hot mess dangling from a thick, twisted chain. The pendant also served as my portal passkey to the other side and perhaps more importantly, my ticket home, so as much as I loathed its appearance, it was kind of a keeper. My remaining pockets were stuffed with healthy snacks as my previous excursion into the afterlife had proven it was better to be prepared than run the risk of being left with no alternative except the consumption of questionably monochromatic food products, assuming there were any to be found. I do not do my best work on an empty stomach.

"Too much?" I bit my lip and glanced down

worriedly at my kick-ass afterlife attire. I knew it looked good. On the other hand, it was also three hundred and sixty degrees away from what I normally wore, and I wouldn't want the unexpected shock to cause anyone permanent damage. "Maybe I should stick with my jeans and tennis shoes and add a shiny cape and a nice tiara?"

"Uh, no…no. You just look…different, that's all," my father replied. "You have a tiara?"

"Life is all about change, Daddy," I pronounced as though I was the first person on Earth who'd ever come to that profound conclusion.

My Dad's bushy salt and pepper eyebrows tangled together over the bridge of his nose. "Who are you, and what have you done with my daughter?"

"It's Denise's fault," I assured him.

"Oh, well, that makes sense." He grimaced.

"You look very nice, dear," Stepmother Gail added with a decisive nod. "That blue really makes your eyes pop."

Judging by the expression currently sported by my father, the Hardware King, something was making his eyes pop, too. Since his eyes were brown, I didn't think it was the color of my shirt.

"You look freakin' hot!" Denise cried happily, clapping her hands together in glee, momentarily forgetting the impressionable young ears of my lovely twin nieces, Mick and Vick, were perked up like rabid elves as they devoted their undivided attention to the entire exchange. Suddenly cognizant of their identical blonde curiosity, she hurried to add. "I mean, the weather is so unpredictable in March. I hope you won't be too warm in that jacket."

"Maybe I should just run home and put my jeans back on," I decided, suddenly not quite as comfortable with the whole life-is-about-change thing as I'd been a few minutes ago. I mean, what if the Grim Reaper took my sudden interest in suburban biker chic as an indication I was trying to impress him or something? Because, I mean, I totally wasn't. I had chosen this ensemble from a purely practical perspective.

The pants practically, you know, made my butt look awesome.

"Don't even think about it," Denise cried, jumping from her chair and flinging herself between me and the door. "You just plant your cowhide covered butt in a chair until Morgan gets here."

"Morgan," shouted Vick.

"Morgan!" echoed Mick.

And before I could make an escape, as though conjured from the mists of time by the fervent shrieks of three natural blondes in rapid succession, there was a crunch of gravel, the slamming of a door, and Morgan Kane in all his Grim Reaper-ish glory filled the doorway. His massive form blocked the light, yet somehow he exuded a particularly attractive light of his own.

"Wow! You do know you're a Retriever and not a vampire, right? How many head of cattle you figure made the ultimate sacrifice for that outfit?" Kane arched a brow in my direction, crossed his arms over his massive flannel-covered chest, and looked me up and down slowly. Very slowly.

"Why, thank you, Kane. You look very nice, too." I sniffed. Killjoy. I wasn't the least bit disappointed the first words out of his mouth weren't *Hell, Logan, you look positively ass-tastick in those pants*. Really. On the other hand, my vulnerable pre-pubescent nieces were avidly observing our exchange, so perhaps he planned to share that particular observation with me later.

Yeah, I was going with that.

"Besides, there's no such thing as vampires."

He raised one perfectly arched brow—his absolute perfection was starting to get on my last nerve—letting me know perhaps my supposition that vampires were creatures relegated solely to Hollywood horror flicks and libido-stimulating novels was an erroneous one.

Well, isn't that special?

"Well, you're apparently ready for anything including the potential threat of road rash, so let's get going, shall we?"

"You know Kane, anyone who wears fur as often as you do should definitely not be making fun of my leather." I mean, the man spent half of his time as a big, black, wolf-like Hellhound. Who was he to ridicule my awesome, figure enhancing, supernatural, superhero gear?

"Touché. Ready, Princess Sassy Pants?" The corners of his lips twitched, and my train of thought jumped the track and passed right by the station.

Hey, it happens. And obviously, he'd noticed the pants and thus, by extension, my ass.

"I suppose." I sighed dramatically, turning my back to the Grim Reaper. Facing my family, I casually knocked one of Vick's pink plastic ponies from the edge of the table. "Oops! My bad."

Carefully bending from the waist to retrieve it from the floor in one well-orchestrated snatch and grab, I presented Morgan Kane with a complete and unobstructed view of my cowhide enhanced derriere. Plopping the pony in front of my niece and ruffling her blonde hair affectionately, I darted a glance at Kane from the corner of my eye to gauge his reaction. He recovered his composure almost immediately, but I knew that look, and his train of thought took an unexpected side trip for a minute, too. Denise, who of course had perfected the very move I'd just made by her junior year in high school, quickly lifted her coffee cup to her lips to hide her grin.

My father clasped and unclasped his hands, cleared his throat, and lowered his shaggy brows.

"Explain to me again why Maxine should risk anything for this little shit. He got himself into this mess, and he managed to kill my daughter and negate the binding of her supernatural superpowers along the way."

Morgan Kane sucked in a deep breath that whistled through his perfectly white teeth, glanced in my direction, and blew it back out again before answering.

"You know how this works. You also know supernatural screw-ups are few and far between and Max won't be called upon all that often. I'd get him out myself if I could, but you know my powers only offer a one way ticket. That being said, I can tag along and do my best to mitigate any danger while Max retrieves the little shit in question. C'mon, he's just a kid, Dan."

"Do you really have superpowers, Aunt Max?" The wide blue eyes of Mick fixed upon me with a gaze of reverent awe. Her identical golden sister Vick wore a similarly impressed expression.

"Um…" Though I knew it was concern prompting his question, I frowned at my father for his indiscretion in mentioning the S-word in front of the girls.

"Why, sure she does, honey," Denise interjected with a smirk. "Aunt Max can eat six donuts in a single sitting and wash them down with a gallon of coffee."

"Oh, that," scoffed Vick as their two cherubic faces fell. "Well, that's nothing special."

"Yeah, well can you do it?" I retorted peevishly while pushing out my lower lip in a pout.

Hey, some of us have limited talents and have to guard them rabidly from potential usurpers.

With a toss of her golden curls, Vick gathered up her toys and stomped off to the den closely followed by her partner in crime. As soon as they were out of earshot, my father turned to me with his brow puckered in worried creases.

"I still don't like this," he muttered. I stretched up on my toes and planted a kiss on his cheek.

"I'll be fine, Daddy. Morgan said so, right, Morgan?"

Kane's grunt might have been one of assent, but frankly, I had the distinct impression it was simply a noncommittal acknowledgment of my question designed to reassure my parental unit. While it didn't do much to assuage my own anxiety, it did clear the furrows from my father's brow, and I was grateful.

"You take care of my baby girl, Reaper," Dad warned as I kissed both he and Gail good-bye.

"To tell the truth, Dan, your girl is pretty damn good at taking care of herself." I felt the color rush into my cheeks.

"Since when?" my father and Denise exclaimed in unison. But even the obvious lack of confidence in my abilities expressed by my very own flesh and blood didn't quench the warm glow suffusing my whole body at the Grim Reaper's compliment. Then again, it could have been a leather-induced hot flash.

"Well, if you've all finished stroking my ego, I think Morgan's right. Time to go," I said as I leaned over to hug my stepmother. "If I'm not back by tomorrow night, can someone please feed Caesar? You know how cranky he gets if he isn't fed on time."

"Since he's the least friendly animal I've ever encountered, I'm not sure how you can tell the difference, but yeah, I'll feed him," Dad groused. "Of course he could survive a week on the fat stored in his tail alone."

Caesar wasn't even close to the least friendly animal I'd ever encountered, but since I was about to return to the place where I was most likely to run into those that were, I wisely refrained from mentioning it.

See how thoughtful I've become?

Kane opened the screen door and stepped out onto the back porch. He stood there holding it open for me, clearly indicating it was time to leave.

Have I mentioned how subtle the man can be?

Plastering a stoic smile on my face, I gave my father another encouraging squeeze and stepped through the door. I reached the truck first and climbed in while Kane loped around to the other side and jumped in the driver's seat with a faint grin quirking up the corners of his mouth. Turning the key, he gunned the engine and peeled out of the drive in reverse.

"I didn't want to say anything in front of your family, Logan...but that outfit does things to me. My mouth is dry, my hands are shaky...hell, I think my heart is beating double time." He glanced at me from the corner of his bright green eyes.

"Really?" My face slowly split into a satisfied grin as my chest expanded, and I fought down the urge to fist pump. I knew he wouldn't be able to resist remarking on the awesomeness that was my ass in these pants indefinitely.

"Hell, yeah! I always get excited by the smell of new truck."

My head swiveled in his direction as my mouth fell open. I mean, I wasn't crushed or anything. Well, okay, maybe I was a *little* crushed. His shoulders shook, and I was so put out that this time I barely noticed how wide and muscular they were. I found myself at a loss for words.

What? It happens.

Of course, historically it doesn't last very long. And you know what they say about history. It always repeats itself. Who was I to buck tradition?

"Stop the truck."

"What?"

"Stop. The. Truck. I want to go home. You think you can show up out of the blue expecting my help after a year of ignoring me, and then just insult me? Well, sorry, Mr. Kane. That's not how I roll." I tried to cross my arms over my chest to punctuate that I meant business, but the leather sleeves of my jacket bunched up and stuck together halfway toward the miffed pose I was aiming for. I clasped my hands together in my lap like a well-behaved Catholic school girl at mass, instead. Yeah, that's right, Reaper...this is what pissed off looks like in Max-land.

Kane surrendered any attempt to hide his amusement and burst out laughing.

"I wasn't insulting you, Logan. I was simply busting your balls."

"Clearly it has escaped your notice, but I am a woman. I do not have balls," I forced out through stiff, offended lips.

"Believe me, the fact you're a woman hasn't escaped my notice for a second. But you're wrong about the balls. You have the biggest set of any woman I know." The grin never left his face, and he continued to barrel along the interstate, making no attempt to stop the vehicle as I had so politely requested.

"You say that like it's a good thing," I grumbled.

"It is," he replied enigmatically, dropping his hand onto the turn signal as our exit appeared ahead. Looking around, it was difficult to reconcile the dissimilarity of the current scenery to that which I'd experienced on my last visit to the Grim Reaper. Sure the trees were still bleak and bare, but if I looked closely, I could discern hints of green where tiny buds struggled to emerge, a drastic change from the heavy burden of snow they'd been groaning under when I saw them last. If I were prone to philosophical thinking—something no one's accused me of in recent memory, or ever—I might interpret these subtle signs of renewal as some cosmic confirmation that nothing stays the same, seasons change, the world moves on, and now I'd moved on, too.

I mean, c'mon, I was barreling down the interstate in a four by four driven by the Grim Reaper on my way to rescue a snot-nosed kid who I didn't even like. Wearing leather.

Of course, I'm pretty sure the powers that be have more pressing issues on their plate than providing me with an understated thumbs-up in my successful navigation of the bereaved state. And maybe I didn't need one. Sure, it took me a while to see the bigger picture—*tell me this surprises you*—but though Roger will always occupy a special place in my heart, I finally understood that moving on doesn't mean forgetting him. It means learning to stop tripping over things that are behind me.

Hey, I know I may not be the brightest star in the sky, but every once in a while I do twinkle.

"You're awfully quiet, Logan," Morgan Kane observed as he swung the nose of the truck into his driveway. The rustic log cabin hadn't changed since I'd driven away from it on the day Roger died. Well, except for the fact there were no ten foot snow drifts and there were at least a dozen flowering dogwoods in full bloom. At the risk of being redundant, flowering dogwoods were the odd avocation of the Grim Reaper.

"Do you make a habit of looking a gift horse in the mouth?" I retorted.

"Point taken," he laughed, green eyes twinkling and white teeth flashing. At least he didn't shrug those shoulders. "However, when the voices in your head suddenly stop projecting out of your mouth, I can't help wondering what the little suckers are up to."

"Actually," I said with an offended sniff. "I was just reflecting on how much growth I've attained as a person and wondering why in the hell I was putting my life on the line for the poster child for contraception. I mean, c'mon. There are a lot of screwed up kids in the world, and no one is heading into the afterlife to save them from their own mistakes. What's so special about this particular kid?"

Morgan Kane turned slightly in his seat and rested his muscular forearm on top of the steering wheel fixing his unnerving green gaze on me at the same time. Then he shrugged.

Wide shoulders, big muscles, yeah, yeah, we've already established I noticed, okay? Sue me.

"You're right, Logan. There are a lot of screwed-up kids in the world, and sadly, too many of them don't have anyone who's even willing to cross the street to save them, let alone cross the veil between life and death. However, none of those kids have Buddy's potential."

He reached for his door handle and hopped to the ground, jogging around the front of the truck to yank my door open while I was still struggling to unbuckle my seat belt, all the while telling myself the sweat slicking my palms was in anticipation of crossing over to the other side. It had nothing whatsoever to do with those shoulders. Nope, nothing at all.

"Really?" I struggled to keep my tone neutral.

Have I mentioned that Buddy was the living, breathing incompetent responsible for my untimely death and subsequent initiation into the supernatural superhero club?

It was particularly difficult for me to ascribe a single redeeming quality to the weasel, let alone identify any potential.

Kane swatted my hands away and released the belt with a flick of his long fingers. I did not for a single second contemplate whether or not his expertise extended to bra hooks.

"Yep, really," he replied with that faint smile playing around the corners of his lips. "And while I believe every kid deserves to be saved, Buddy is kind of a special case. You see, he isn't one of those kids who, if left to his own devices, will grow up to rob convenience stores or get involved with drugs. Nasty stuff, sure, but realistically impacting a limited number of people. Buddy-gone-bad has a much broader reach. You see, Buddy has the ability to cause the Zombie Apocalypse."

Chapter 11

Zombie Apocalypse? You would think by this time, I would have flushed any and all disbelief down the toilet. I thought I had. Guess what? I was wrong. Until now I'd had no desire whatsoever to stick my neck out for this kid, but if Kane was telling the truth, I guess I had no choice but to consider embracing my mission.

One more time, for the record—why me?

But Buddy in the role of the Zombie Master? Given his track record thus far, I was relatively certain absolutely no good could come from that scenario.

"What choo talkin' 'bout, Reaper?" I asked as I skidded into the entryway behind him. The soles of my new shit-kicker boots were a bit slick. At least that was the excuse I used for the ungainly slide which caused me to crash into Morgan Kane's broad back necessitating an ass grab to regain my balance. Hey, if a girl's made a decision to embrace life, she may as well start with something well worth embracing, right?

In case you were wondering, it was just as scrumptiously round and firm as it looked.

"At such a loss for words you've taken to impersonating seventies sitcom characters?" Kane turned his head ever so slightly to peer over his shoulder and glance down at my fingers enthusiastically clutching his ass. I reluctantly released his firm and globular buttocks and laced my fingers together in front of me.

"Do not hate on the pre-millennial classics of comedy," I sniffed, attempting to appear offended. In actuality, I was trying to refrain from grabbing his ass again. I was also contemplating how on earth a slick faced teen with moderate acne, purple braces, and a seemingly limitless ability to screw up could possibly be anything as impressive as the Zombie King. Which of course, he couldn't, because everyone knows Zombies are not real.

"Now about this whole Zombie Apocalypse thing…" I began primly. Morgan Kane turned to face me and tucked his a loose strand of his long, dark hair behind the ragged remains of his left ear. I hadn't noticed it earlier. I craned my neck to get a better look. "Your scars are gone, why didn't your ear heal, too?"

"Distractible much?" He reached out and cupped his long fingers around the nape of my neck, propelling me in the direction of the kitchen. The warmth of his fingers sent a shiver of sensation racing from the base of my skull all the way down to the bottom of my spine. I'm pretty sure my toes curled within the snug leather confines of my lovely new boots. Truthfully, I was finding the Grim Reaper increasingly distracting the longer I was in his company. Of course, there was no reason to share that with him, although the gleam in his arresting green eyes hinted he might already suspect. Some people move on by dipping a toe hesitantly into the shallow end of the kiddie pool. I apparently cliff dive. It was entirely possible I was in big trouble. Sadly, it wasn't a new experience for me.

"C'mon, Logan, let's talk about Buddy over a cup

of coffee. It's been at least an hour since you fed your caffeine addiction. I don't need you going all ape-shit crazy before we even get started."

"Do you have doughnuts?"

"Nope." His fingers squeezed my neck lightly before he dropped his hand to capture mine and drag me the remaining distance to the kitchen. It was as lovely as I remembered with its high beamed ceiling, wide planked pine floors, and U-shaped granite countertop. At the far side of the room, a fire blazed cheerily in the large, fieldstone fireplace. I thought it was terribly negligent of him to have left it burning while he was out, but given his origins in the suburbs of Hell, I figured he knew his way around a fire better than most.

He pulled out one of the mismatched chairs around the weathered farmhouse table and pushed me into it before moving around the breakfast bar to start the coffee. For such a large man, he navigated the java preparation area with an efficient economy of movement. That led me to believe he did this often. Perhaps his coffee consumption was on a par with my own, which honestly increased his appeal in my book. While the coffee brewed, filling the kitchen with the aroma of heaven, he rummaged in a cabinet, tugging out a crumpled brown paper bag. After pouring a cup for each of us, he hooked a finger through the handles of both and plunked one down in front of me, sliding the other and the paper bag to his own seat. Apparently remembering how I preferred my poison, he didn't offer the sugar bowl. He stepped back to the fridge to retrieve the cow shaped pottery creamer and set it within my reach before he dropped into his chair.

I tipped the creamer, allowing the cow to spew a dollop into my cup, then raised the cup to my lips, took a large sip, and closed my eyes in ecstatic appreciation. The Hellhound really was a coffee brewing god.

"Now about Buddy and the Zombies," he took a sip and set his cup on the table with a clunk.

"Morgan, everyone knows there are no such things as Zombies."

Okay so everyone also knew there was no such thing as Laminae hookers, or three-headed guardians of the gates of Hell, or shape-shifting Hellhounds, either. Right? Yeah, well, I'd already had that prettily woven rug pulled unceremoniously from beneath my fugly booted feet. I knew he was going to prove me wrong, but I was desperate to cling to my delusions just a while longer.

Seriously, can you blame me?

"Oh sure," I continued with an edge of desperation in my voice that was apparent even to my own ears. "There was that case involving a man who died in a Haitian hospital in 1962, was pronounced dead by two different doctors, and was buried. Then he walked up to his sister in a rural village in 1980 and introduced himself. While you might argue that's potential proof Zombies exist, you should know research determined it was most likely his experience was the result of complete faith in *bokor* sorcery and the use of complex powders made from dried and ground plants and animals. Still pretty impressive, but hardly supernatural."

"Do tell." Kane leaned back in his chair, stretched his long legs out in front of him, and brought his cup to his lips, hiding the faint smile I saw hovering there.

"Well, yeah," I continued stubbornly. I was not buying into Buddy the Zombie Master without a fight. "And if one subscribes to the theory Zombies are by definition will-less, speechless, reanimated human corpses, let me just point out that guy went on to resume his life and even have children after his miraculous return from the grave. I'm pretty sure I've never heard of a single dead guy who can procreate."

"Good point." He gave up any attempt to hide his amusement and set the cup back on the table, leaning forward in my direction. "Tell me, Logan. What other useless trivia do you have clattering around in that pretty head of yours?"

Pretty? I blinked. He thought I was pretty? Well, apparently he though my head was pretty at least. It was a start. But I digress.

"And just for the record, there's no evidence he ever snacked on human brains, either. Seriously, how ridiculous is that anyway? I mean, c'mon, the human brain is relatively small, more protected, and less accessible than any other organ in the human body. What self-respecting and hungry Zombie wants to work so hard for so little? If Zombies were real, it would be far more sensible and satisfying to gnaw on a chunky butt or thunder thigh. Don't you think?"

"So you've got this whole Zombie thing all figured out, huh?" He arched a dark brow and leaned back.

"Probably not." I chuffed out a resigned sigh. "But it was worth a shot."

"Has anyone ever mentioned you have a particularly well-developed talent for rationalization?"

"Not lately, but there have been rumors."

"Sorry to burst your well-researched and artfully

articulated bubble, but Zombies do indeed exist."

"Of course they do. Couldn't you just lie once in a while and let me wallow in my naiveté?"

"Well, I guess I could, but it wouldn't change the facts in the long run. Besides, your reactions are always so entertaining." He laughed.

Entertaining and pretty? Things were looking up. Now if he would just compliment my ass, my work here would be done.

"So what do you think of my pants?"

Yes, I asked.

I threw it right out there like a cookie and waited for him to bite. The cookie, not my ass, although I was game for either.

"We're discussing the possibility of the end of life as we know it, and you're fishing for compliments?"

"Depends."

"On?"

"Whether or not you're biting. A situation is never so dire a girl does not welcome an ego boost."

"Fine. Your ass is positively edible in those pants. From past experience, I can also confirm I find it much the same, and perhaps even more so, out of them. Now, can we get back to the business at hand? We've got bigger problems."

"Problems? You think being attracted to my ass is a problem?"

"Try to focus, Logan. Lives depend upon it."

"Right. Buddy and the Zombie Apocalypse. " I sat up straighter in my chair and took another slug of coffee determined to give him my full attention. Morgan Kane thought I was pretty and entertaining and thought my ass was edible. Things were looking up.

Well, except for the whole prospect of a Zombie Apocalypse.

"Have you ever heard of the field of neuroparasitology?"

"Something to do with parasites of the nervous system?"

"You knew that?" While I would have been quite happy to bask in Morgan Kane's clear admiration of my superior intelligence, I didn't want to give him the impression I was one of those socially challenged and frigid brainy types. Because I so wasn't. Frigid, I mean. Or brainy. Socially challenged? Well, two out of three isn't bad, right?

"Word roots. Lucky guess," I conceded with a sigh. "Anyway, what does that have to do with Buddy and Zombies?"

"What if I told you the potential for Zombie conversion already exists in a large percentage of the world's population, both living and dead?"

"That's impossible," I muttered under my breath.

"You're a formerly dead Retriever sitting here having coffee with the Grim Reaper who also happens to be a shape-shifting Hellhound, and you're really going to go there?"

"Let me rephrase that." I sighed. "How is that possible?"

"Influenza," he announced.

"Come again?" I narrowed my eyes and screwed up my face as I tried to figure out what the hell he was talking about. Then I realized it probably wasn't an attractive look and, loathe to have him suddenly begin re-evaluating his previous assessment of the prettiness of my head, I forcibly relaxed my features.

"Influenza," he said again. "You know, seasonal flu."

"German measles."

"What?"

"Chickenpox. Aren't we playing Name That Illness? Do I win? Are there prizes?"

"For the love of...Logan, this isn't a game." He yanked at the elastic band holding his hair back, then raked his fingers through it before shaking it out with even more agitation than he had earlier. It settled around his shoulders—his broad, muscular shoulders—in a dark cloud framing his face. I was trying to pay attention, I swear. But between the hair shaking and shoulder shrugging, I had my work cut out for me. If he flashed a glimpse of that ass, I would not be responsible for the consequences.

"Do you think you can concentrate for five minutes?" He glared across the table in my direction.

"Well, I'll try, but you'll have to promise not to shrug, shake your head, or bend over."

He drew in a deep breath and opened his mouth, then snapped his lips together and rolled his eyes. He pinched the bridge of his nose between his thumb and forefinger, closed his eyes, and—I could be mistaken—but I'm pretty sure I heard him count to ten under his breath.

"Okay, imagine an organism enters a victim. Typically the immune system kicks in and releases substances to fight the infestation causing the host to feel sick."

"Infection...yeah, okay that makes sense." I nodded. "But what does it have to do with Buddy the Zombie King?"

"I'm getting to it," he growled. "Sometimes the organism manages to mutate or find a way to manipulate the host's immune system to escape destruction."

"On the order of antibiotic resistant bacteria," I nodded again, getting the gist.

Hey, I was married to a doctor for thirteen years. He may have been a proctologist and not an epidemiologist, but let's face it, colons are not immune to bacteria, and a girl overhears things.

"Exactly. But some organisms have taken things an evolutionary step further. They don't simply manipulate the victim's immune system in order to survive, they manipulate it into producing modulators that change behavior. For example, there's a species of worm that needs to get inside a sheep to reproduce. It infects and hijacks the brain of a certain species of ant, programming it to climb to the top of a blade of grass and stay there until the grass is eaten by the sheep. The parasite hijacks the ant's nervous system, effectively turning it into a Zombie."

"No offense Morgan, but while it might be creepy, little tiny ant zombies windsurfing on a blade of grass waiting to be eaten isn't exactly the stuff of which horror movies are made."

"Somehow I think the ants might disagree," he smirked. "Anyway, that was just an example to demonstrate the concept. To compound the problem, a lot of these organisms tend to favor the brain because it shelters them from the full fury of the immune system while giving them full access to the mainframe for the alteration of behavior."

Now it was my turn to pinch my nose between my

thumb and forefinger and close my eyes as it all began to come together in my mind like a lump of cold oatmeal. I suddenly feared I knew exactly where this was going, and my stomach churned as the fog dissipated and the big picture took shape.

"You're telling me the influenza virus carries a parasite that burrows into the brains of every person who's ever been infected?" I glanced up to find Kane staring at me intently.

He nodded slowly. "The parasites remain dormant, unless activated, at which time they begin to reproduce and modulate the host behavior."

"Putting the host under the control of the parasite, just like a Zombie. And the parasite is activated and under the control of…?"

"Your friend, Buddy."

Chapter 12

"This is so not the kind of news you should spring on a girl unless there are doughnuts," I groused. I mean, okay, I realize fried dough stuffed with raspberry jam and covered in white frosting and coconut wouldn't prevent the Zombie Apocalypse, but honestly, I was pretty sure it couldn't make things any worse, either. And it would sure as hell make *me* feel better. "And at the risk of being redundant, may I reiterate for the record that Buddy is no friend of mine?"

"Okay, so I don't have doughnuts, but I did get you these. Forgiven?" Kane pushed the crinkled paper bag across the table with an expectant gleam in his eye.

"You bought something for me?" I pulled the bag closer and peered inside, spying a cellphone bag filled with small brown pellets.

"You bought me a bag of rabbit poop?" Tugging the cellophane free. I turned it over and read the label. Chocolate Covered Arabica Beans. I quickly unzipped the pocket of my jacket and tossed the dry-as-a-fart granola bars on the table, replacing them with my new nuggets of nirvana.

"Thank you." I knew my smile was far brighter than a pocket-sized sack of snack food warranted, but c'mon. The Grim Reaper bought me chocolate...and coffee...all rolled up together in tiny portable bites. He was obviously as perceptive and brilliant as he was stunning.

"You're welcome. You did bring your necklace, didn't you?"

"Yeah, it's in my pocket, but if we're going together, I don't really need it, right?"

"We're going in together. Whether we come out together remains to be seen. I may have slightly exaggerated Cerberus' willingness to relinquish Buddy without a fight." He avoided my gaze, suddenly very interested in the crackling flames of the fire. "I'm sure things will be fine, but you might want to put it on."

"So you lied?"

"I prefer to think of it as strategically redirecting the truth."

"Yeah well, I prefer to think of myself as statuesque, but it doesn't make me any taller."

"Look, Cerberus thrives on mayhem. What better way to achieve it than to have someone with Buddy's abilities under his thumb? So yeah, he won't give him up willingly, but I intend to get him back, just the same."

"But if Buddy signed on with the dark side of his own free will, what makes you think he'll be open to being saved?"

Even as I asked, I knew he was open to it. In fact, thinking back to the last time I'd seen him, I was pretty sure he wasn't just willing to be rescued, he was desperate.

"From the moment he was born and it was clear who and what he was, the supernatural community has been trying to find an alternate role for him, one that would make him happy while reducing the risk of his acting on his abilities. Problem is, he just doesn't seem to be good at anything."

"Did anyone ever ask *him*?"

"Huh?"

"Did anyone ever bother to ask Buddy what he wanted to do? Or did you all just assume you knew what was best for him? Maybe he's never been good at anything because you've all been try to fit a square peg in a round hole."

"How could he know what was best? He's just a kid." Kane straightened in his chair and glared at me across the table.

"May I refresh your memory?" I raised a brow in inquiry and held up a finger. I took Kane's annoyed expression as an affirmative. "Please recall the mind-numbing, eyeball-gouging educational session on psychology with my sister to which you subjected me earlier today. Buddy is a teenager. If you really buy into the whole theory I was forced to endure for the better part of an hour this morning, he's at the stage where he's taking his first tentative steps toward independence, seeking a sense of self. Identity versus confusion. If everyone around him is boxing him into the identity *they* think he should assume, how is he ever supposed to have a sense of self or a feeling of independence and control? The way I see it, you've all been setting him up for failure bound to result in insecurity and confusion on his part. Did it ever occur to you that maybe he signed up with your bigger, uglier cousin because it's the first decision he's been allowed to make for himself? A bad decision, I'll grant you, but at least it was all his own."

"Well…shit!" Kane slumped in his chair and tossed back the remainder of his coffee.

Have I mentioned it was really, really good coffee?

Frankly, I suspected he was now too distracted to fully appreciate its awesomeness, and I momentarily regretted sharing my temporary flash of brilliance before he'd had a chance to savor the last drop.

"Okay, well in my defense, I haven't had a helluva lot of experience with kids."

"Well, this isn't all on you, right? I mean, the kid's got family. They have to assume some accountability in this mess."

"You've met Marvin and Melvin. You honestly think they have a clue what to do with someone like Buddy? They're a couple of disorganized lower level bureaucrats who, though they mean well, aren't exactly role model material."

"Parents?" I asked hopefully.

"Dead." Ah, hell. Of course they were. Why would there be any hope I could just bring the kid out and dump him on someone's doorstep. Kane rose to his impressive height and snatched my empty cup from under my nose, carrying it to the sink along with his own. Then he turned back to face me, cocked a hip against the counter, and crossed his arms over his chest. His broad, muscular chest.

Not that I noticed.

"What do you think, Logan? You up for it?"

Was I up for playing surrogate mom to a confused teenage Zombie King with an attitude? Doubtful. Don't get me wrong, I love kids. It's just that before I discovered I couldn't have them, I always figured I'd get to screw them up myself, not be saddled with trying to straighten out someone else's sloppy seconds.

"Probably not, but I guess I can't do any worse

with him than everyone else already has, right?"

"Okay, let's go with that." It struck me he hadn't actually agreed with me, but I didn't have time to think up a witty comeback as he strode across the kitchen and yanked me out of my chair. Dragging me behind him, he headed for the gothic monstrosity that passed as his office where he kept the large oval mirror which would serve as our portal to the Between.

The room hadn't changed since my last visit. The shiny scythe still glinted from its spot in the corner. Dark heavy drapes still hung at the windows, obscuring the world outside, and the furniture was just as dark and heavy. I glanced at the row of small, potted dogwood trees growing along one wall and couldn't understand how they managed to survive in the sunless gloom. Of course, the one at my place still hadn't died and that might be an even bigger miracle.

As soon as we crossed the threshold, Kane released my hand and headed for the corner, dragging the mirror from its place. He positioned the mirror in the middle of the room and straightened, motioning me closer with a smile. Even with the distracting scars, his smile was enough to jump-start the libido of any normal woman. And now that he'd healed…well, fortunately, as we've already determined, I am not a normal woman.

I, of course, was immune.

"Put your necklace on, Logan." He stepped back from the mirror and dusted his hands down the sides of his jeans. Rolling my eyes, I fished the fugly thing from my pocket and dropped it over my head. It bounced against my underwire assisted breasts as heavy and ostentatious as ever—the necklace, not my breasts, which we have already established trend toward the modest end of the hoo-ha scale—but the action succeeded in drawing Kane's gaze to my chest where it lingered a fraction of second longer than warranted. How do I know he wasn't simple admiring my taste in golden baubles? Because his eyes didn't budge even after I yanked out the neckline of my T-shirt and dropped the offending item inside and out of sight. And then his tongue snaked out to lick his lips. Score!

"You ready?" His voice sounded oddly hoarse.

"Hell, no," I snapped back, stepping closer to where he waited near the mirror. "But that's never stopped me before."

"As I said earlier, biggest balls of any woman I know. Yours just happen to be on your chest," he laughed, laying one hand on the surface of the mirror and reaching for mine with the other. The cool, silver sheen of the mirror slowly changed and morphed into a thick, swirling vortex of opaque gray fog, just as it had on the previous occasion when I'd touched my fugly necklace to it. I was a little jealous the Grim Reaper didn't need to rely on questionable fashion accessories to come and go as he pleased.

Glancing down at my girls with a frown before grabbing his outstretched hand, I said, "Yeah well, if you're referring to these, perhaps you should rethink your descriptor. Big isn't exactly the first word that comes to mind."

"You know what they say, Logan." He laughed, picking up a boot clad foot and thrusting one leg through the mirror and into the fog. "More than a mouthful is simply a waste."

I was glad he'd already disappeared into the afterlife and wasn't there to witness my jaw hitting the floor. Gaping is such an unattractive look. I would have loved to stand there pondering his remark for a few minutes.

Can you blame me?

My fantasy, however, was rudely interrupted by the impatient tug on my hand reminding me we had work to do. Yeah, the Grim Reaper and I were about to get busy, and not in a good way. With a sigh, I squared my shoulders, took a deep breath, and stepped into the great beyond.

Unlike the last time I'd stepped through the mirror and into the shifting curtain of murky vapor, no creepy little tendrils unwound from the soupy mist to crawl over my skin like living things. As we stepped clear of the mist into the central square of gray, the Lost also failed to congregate around me for a quick grope. Last time I'd been here, they rushed to crowd me in a desperate, sightless throng plucking at my clothes and giving me a major case of the heebs. The Timekeeper had told me that craving life, they were attracted to my mortal energy. Apparently, Kane's swirling aura of death trumped my bright, shiny glow of life, because this time, they gave us a wide berth, and in a few cases they even crossed the street to avoid us. This, of course, gave us an unobstructed path to the Timekeeper's front porch. Bonus!

I squinted through the grayness and there she was, exactly where she'd been on my last foray into the sweet hereafter. The old woman sat on the porch of a tiny cottage set back from the street swaying to and fro in a creaky, wooden rocking chair, two long knitting needles clacking in her gnarled and twisted fingers. Her tiny, twinkling eyes observed us from a face as wrinkled and desiccated as a dried apple topped by a mop of wispy, white candy-floss hair. She was the Timekeeper, or as I had come to think of her, Granny-Apple-Head.

I realized Morgan Kane still gripped my hand within his own larger, warmer one when I managed to navigate the stairs without prostrating myself at the Timekeeper's feet as I'd done on my prior visit.

Hey, anyone can fall down stairs, falling up stairs takes skill.

Granny-Apple-Head smiled as we approached, twitching aside the endless pile of worsted wool spilling along the porch deck and over the railing, to reveal two additional chairs. She released the knitting needles and lumbered to her feet, and just like the last time I was here, the damn things kept right on clacking away with no assistance from her. Knit one, purl two...time marches on. She'd explained it all to me before, but seeing it up close and personal still made the hair on the back of my neck spring to attention.

"Mabel." Kane released my hand, and then he leaned forward to kiss Granny-Apple-Head's papery cheek. "Always nice to see you."

"Well, of course it is," she cackled, patting his arm affectionately before fixing her gleaming raisin-like peepers on me. "Hello, Maxine. You're looking well."

"Hi, uh thanks. You're looking..."

Have I mentioned she resembled a wrinkled and desiccated piece of fruit topped by a mop of wispy, white candy-floss hair?

"You, uh, haven't changed a bit."

See? Every now and then, my if-you-can't-say-something-nice gene kicks in. Stepmother Gail would be so proud.

"One of the perks of the job." She winked, lowering herself back to the rocker and taking up her knitting. "I presume you're here to retrieve the boy?"

"Always one step ahead of me." Kane grinned. "You know where I can find him?"

"Of course I know where you can find him, but you don't need me to tell you that. You know as well as I do." She glanced up from beneath wrinkled eyelids with a sly expression. "Have to say I'm a little surprised you'd consider taking Maxine along."

"Actually, I was going to ask if you'd mind if she hung out here with you while I go in. I'll send Buddy back here so she can get him out."

Her meaty shoulders rose and fell in a shrug. "Okay by me. Had a hunch I might be getting company. Baked cookies."

While there's nothing I love more than being talked about as though I'm not there, followed closely by having my decisions made for me, I felt compelled to say something.

Don't tell me this surprises you.

"Um, yeah. While I've never been a girl to turn my nose up at empty calories, I'll have to pass on the baked goods." I tugged on Kane's sleeve until he looked down into my eyes. Reluctantly, I thought. "This was not the plan. Therefore, I'll be sticking with you, Big Guy. Like stink on garbage."

Chapter 13

"Logan," the Grim Reaper began in a patronizing tone that strongly reminded me of an adult trying to reason with a small child. "If you'll think back, we never discussed any specific plan."

"I see. Another strategic redirection of the truth?" I snapped. What was it with these people? Could they never simply lay their cards on the table? "So let me get this straight. After a year of ignoring my existence, you show up at my father's, eat my doughnuts, subject me to a long winded dissertation on Erikson's theory of psychosocial development, and coerce me into hoofing it into the Between to save Buddy. Which, by the way, Denise then construes as a date necessitating a shopping trip resulting in a maxed out credit card and my ass in a pair of leather pants. Now you expect me to just sit here twiddling my thumbs, nibbling monochromatic cookies washed down with indigestion-inducing lemonade while you head off into danger all by yourself to save the day?"

Yes, I said that all in one breath. Impressed?

"Well, sure it sounds bad when you say it like that." Kane's green eyes twinkled, though he had enough sense of self-preservation not to crack a smile. "And I wasn't ignoring your existence, I was respecting your grief and giving you time to move on."

"I'm sorry, dear, I'm all out of lemonade. Afraid it

will have to begin this time," Granny-Apple-Head interjected with a smirk.

"Tempting as that sounds, I'm going with the Hellhound here," I insisted, locking eyes with Kane, planting my hands on my hips, and barely resisting the urge to stomp my foot. Wait a minute...he wasn't ignoring me?

"Hey." Kane dropped his hands to my shoulders and pulled me around in front of him so that we were face to face. "If I could have gotten the kid over to the other side myself, I would have never even involved you in this. Where I'm going and what I may have to do to get him back is not something I ever wanted you to see."

"Why?"

"Why?" He gazed off somewhere over my head, and his jaw clenched tightly enough to snap teeth. "Because there's a good chance there will be a fight. And if there's a fight, I'll have to shift."

"Yeah, so?" He continued to stare off into space, his green eyes glowing with something I couldn't quite decipher.

"Yeah so, I would rather not have you...see me like that," he muttered. I felt my eyebrows lift into my hairline. Impossible as it was to believe, it appeared the Grim Reaper was a little self-conscious. Did he honestly think seeing his animal form would somehow diminish my opinion of him? Judging by the expression on his face, that was exactly what he thought. Clearly, he had short-term memory issues.

"Morgan?" I laid my hands on his bulging biceps and curled my nails into his flesh until he deigned to meet my gaze. "I already saw you, remember? The first time we met."

Lost, frozen, and near death, I owed my life to that big, black Hellhound. Sure, I'd initially thought he was a wolf with all those big, pointy teeth looking like they meant business, but instead of tearing my throat out he'd nudged my cheek and licked my face with his warm, rough tongue, and when I woke up, I was safe in the Grim Reaper's cabin.

"Well, you were pretty much indisposed at the time, so it hardly counts," he grumbled glancing away again.

"Indisposed, incontinent, and incapable of saving myself. If you hadn't shifted to track me, I would be a popsicle, a snow-cone in the woods, a—"

"Okay, I get the point. You would have frozen to death."

"Actually you missed the point entirely. No big surprise. It's an inescapable genetic predisposition of the Y-chromosome. The Hellhound is part of who you are, just as the Carbohydrate Whore is part of who I am. And while that's a line I could have never imagined incorporating into a conversation—ever—the point is, I don't have a problem with it. If anyone in this scenario has the right to be self-conscious, I vote for the incontinent woman with the pee-soaked panties." He'd blown off my embarrassment at the time by explaining it was a body's natural reaction to hypothermia, and it was—I Googled it after the fact just to be sure—still, a girl does hope to make a slightly better first impression.

"You say that now, but you haven't actually seen it. You'd feel differently if you did."

"Who was she?"

His head whipped around, and his gaze locked on

me again as his brows took a trip northward.

"Who was who?"

"The woman who couldn't handle what you were?"

"You have no idea what you're talking about," he muttered with a frown. "And anyway, my shifting isn't the only reason I'd rather you wait here."

"Yeah, I think I do. But the bottom line is, whoever she was, I'm not her. Honestly, I'd have thought you'd have figured that out by now. For better or worse, I'm not your average run of the mill."

His chest expanded—*yeah, I didn't think it was possible for it to get any broader, either*—as he sucked in a deep breath and blew it out slowly. Rubbing his hands briskly up and down my arms, he gazed down at me with a half-smile curling his well-defined, very masculine lips.

"You really are a rather remarkable woman, you know that?" Oh. My. God. He was looking at me the way I look at chocolate.

If you've ever seen me look at chocolate, you'll understand how incredibly significant that is.

My lungs suddenly felt too small to take in sufficient air.

"Preaching to the choir, Reaper," I quipped finally, while a flock of butterflies frantically beat their wings in my throat leaving me breathless. "So are we in this together or do I go home and take up origami?"

"We're in it together," he said after a slight hesitation, and I got the oddest sensation. It could have been caused by the fact I suspected he wasn't talking about the rescue of Buddy the Weasel anymore. Sadly, it was more likely caused by the consumption of one too many cups of coffee before crossing over. I tore my gaze away from Morgan Kane's unnerving stare, and I regarded the Timekeeper who'd been quietly knitting away while observing the entire exchange.

"Do you have a bathroom I could use, by any chance?"

What? It happens.

"Really, Logan?" Kane chuckled. "You couldn't have gone before we left the house?"

"I know, right?" Granny-Apple-Head wheezed back in her raspy voice. "Top of the steps, first door on the left."

Hey, what can I say? Aside from the central nervous system stimulating awesomeness of caffeine, coffee also has an annoying little diuretic side effect. Granted, someone who has reached my level of consumption and maintained it for a lengthy period of time should have developed a tolerance by now, but coupled with a bladder the size of a lima bean, let's just say it's sometimes a challenge.

"Well, I'm assuming there won't be a whole lot of rest stops at which to take a potty break on our upcoming expedition, so I figured I better go now, okay?"

I spun on my heel and yanked open the screen door. I hadn't been in the house before. There was a narrow hallway in front of me leading to the back of the house and a small parlor on my right. It was crammed with more crap than the clearance bin at the dollar store. On every square inch of wall space, and resting on every conceivable surface, was a clock. Big clocks, small clocks, clocks of all styles, shapes, and sizes, tick-tocking in unison at a decibel level that made me feel like I was trapped inside a time bomb. Shoved in between the clocks, in any minute sliver of available space, were balls of yarn in every color and texture imaginable. Well, it was the Timekeeper's house after all, but I couldn't help thinking maybe she'd gone a tad overboard. Shaking my head, I stomped up the stairs, pausing briefly at the top to drag in some air. It really sucks that when I exercise the only thing I seem to lose is my ability to breathe.

The bathroom was a surprise.

Okay, the fact there was a bathroom in the afterlife at all was a surprise, but I figured that was so obvious I didn't need to remark on it.

It kind of reminded me of the one at my Grandma's house when I was a kid. The reek of floral-scented soap was strong enough to curl my nose hairs. The cramped room sported an old-fashioned pedestal sink, a toilet with an overhead pull-chain tank, and a white cast iron claw foot tub, all surrounded with the blinding black and pink tile combination that had been popular somewhere around 1949. I had a sudden, and unwelcome, vision of Mabel the Timekeeper climbing naked into the bath and wondered if there was a bottle of bleach around anywhere to scrub the backs of my eyelids. I was thrilled, however, to discover Granny-Apple-Head apparently had come into a stash of my favorite toilet paper. The kind that was soft and quilted and never, ever had the poor taste to stick to my bottom no matter what it was called upon to absorb. After taking care of business and adjusting my leathers back into place, I reached up and yanked the chain. The loud, screeching sound which accompanied the whirlpool of water swirling down the bowl made me hope, for the Timekeeper's sake, there was a good plumber in the afterlife. Granny's pipes weren't sounding at all healthy. Then I realized the sound was coming from outside the door. The screeching was followed by a loud clunk as the door shuddered from the force of something being settled against it.

What the hell?

I quickly pumped a glob of alcohol hand sanitizer into my palm—*Yeah, don't ask me where she came by that either*—as I am a strong believer that hand hygiene is the key to infection prevention. I rubbed my hands together briskly, yanked open the door, and found myself staring at the back of a tall piece of furniture which blocked my exit.

"Kane?" I rapped my knuckles on the wood. I received no response save a low rumble of laughter from the hallway on the other side of the obstacle. Undeterred, I pounded harder. "Kane, you feaky snucker! Move this hulking behemoth right this second. You said we were in this together!"

"We are in this together, Logan. Together includes me sending Buddy to you as soon as I get him free, and you getting him back to the other side. Together does not include me risking your neck to do it."

"You know what? This strategic redirection of the truth thing you've got going on is really getting on my last nerve. I knew what the risks were when I said I'd help. And if it all goes to hell in a hand-basket, well, at least I'll have died for a noble cause, right? Besides, I went shopping for this. With Denise. I bought leather. That should count for something, Kane. Now move this damn thing and let me out!"

"C'mon, Logan, we both know it's a better bet you'll die by falling up a flight of stairs and choking on a piece of chocolate. I've decided it's too dangerous to take you along, so be a good girl, get the kid home, and behave until I get back. Trust me. The investment in the leather was not wasted. If you play your cards right, I might even, you know, take you out on a date or something after this is all over and done with."

"You've decided? Well, you know what, Kane? Grim Reaper or not, you aren't the boss of me, so just cut the—Wait a minute. Did you say date?" A warm flush of anticipation replaced the hot flush of thoroughly pissed, and suffused me from head to toe. It could have been because I was swathed in leather in a small, confined room with a pathetic lack of ventilation, considering its primary function. But I didn't think that was the reason. Morgan Kane wanted to take me on a date? My eyes widened, my toes curled. I pressed my thighs together and squirmed.

"Well, dinner plans could be rather difficult to coordinate if you're chained to a boulder in Cerberus' dungeon, don't you think?" I huffed.

"He doesn't have an actual dungeon, and I can handle him. By the way, if it will make you feel any better, my cousin isn't *the* Cerberus. The real Cerberus was our great-great grandfather many times removed. Cerberus is actually my cousin's middle name. He just uses it because he has an inflated sense of his own importance. His real name is Harvey."

"Seriously? Like the big invisible rabbit in the 1950s movie classic of the same name?"

"Yep."

"Well, maybe you've forgotten, but I've already met him, and he was anything but cuddly. He seemed pretty damn threatening to me, regardless of his actual name. Please let me out. I…don't want anything to happen to you, either."

He was quiet for so long I was afraid he'd left.

"Reaper?"

"Just watch out for Buddy, and take care of yourself, Logan. I'll see you when I get back."

As his heavy footsteps slowly descended the stairs and faded away, I ground my teeth, and fought the urge to scream. I mean, I would have, but fortunately, I realized in the nick of time that I was trapped in a small, closed space with questionable acoustics and doing so would probably hurt me far more than anyone else. I had to get out of here. Kane had dangled the date carrot. I wanted that date. In fact, I was beginning to think maybe I wanted a whole lot more. As long as he continued to steer clear of plaid polyester golf pants and black cashmere socks, anyway. It was time to dance like no one was watching. Of course, I'd tried that once and someone *was* watching, thought I was having a seizure, and called an ambulance. Wound up in the hospital under observation for two whole days. It was not pretty.

Slamming the commode lid closed, I dropped my leather clad butt on it and looked around. Sink, tub, toilet…sink, tub, toilet, big freaking armoire blocking the door…sink, tub, toilet, big freaking armoire…window. Ha! You have to get up pretty early in the morning to pull one over on Max Logan.

Okay, so maybe you didn't have to get up really early, just sometime before noon, and definitely before I've had my coffee.

But I digress. I jumped to my feet, hitched up my sassy pants, and gripped the sill. I huffed and I puffed for all I was worth, but the damn thing didn't budge. Belatedly, it occurred to me that unlocking it might facilitate the entire process. Unsurprisingly, it did. In case I neglected to mention it earlier, in the afterlife absolutely everything was a nondescript shade of gray. People, houses, animals, plants...there was not a single drop of color to be seen anywhere. Well, except for outsiders like Kane and myself who didn't actually belong here, and the occasional unfortunate D.I.E.s (Death in Error). D.I.E.s managed to retain a faint washed out color hue distinguishing them as souls requiring retrieval. By yours truly. Thankfully, in my admittedly limited supernatural experience, they'd been few and far between. Just between us, I had my fingers crossed that particular trend continued indefinitely.

With a decidedly unladylike grunt, I pushed the sash as high as it would go and then stuck my head out to survey the swirling gray landscape. Just my luck there was neither a downspout nor a rose trellis conveniently propped against the house the way there is in every single movie requiring exit via a second story window. My only hope appeared to be a cluster of fluffy shrubbery positioned just below the window that might break the worst of my fall...er, graceful descent. Damn it, I hate heights. Before I had time to overthink it and scare the crap out of myself, I climbed through the window, dangled from the sill by my fingertips for what seemed like an eternity, swallowed a scream, and let myself drop. The ground was a lot farther than it appeared. Naturally. Oh, and the bushes weren't especially fluffy.

Honestly, I wasn't particularly surprised, either.

I hit the ground feet first, just as I planned. I did

not, however, anticipate the prompt and painful collapse of my knees from the impact, and I went down with a crash. Until the nausea passed, I lay there flat on my back panting. And not in a good way. Tentatively, I moved each separately articulating appendage, and prayed the bushes were the only things that had been broken. Thus reassured I was still in one piece, I sat up cautiously, plucking twigs and leaves from my hair, and concluded I'd live, although the landing was definitely going to leave a mark. Or ten. I climbed stiffly to my feet, congratulating myself on the decision to wear my awesome leather attire, which had protected me from the worst of the herbaceous landscaping. That's me, discovering my superhero abilities, one injury at a time.

And you thought the leather was all about the ass, didn't you?

I limped around to the front of the house. Granny-Apple-Head was still there knitting her fingers to the bone while rocking out to her own demented drummer, but Kane was nowhere in sight. Well, wasn't that inconvenient?

Chapter 14

"I told him it was a stupid idea," Granny grumbled loudly before I'd even cleared the side of the porch. "I knew you'd be too stubborn to stay put, and now I can't even get into my own bathroom."

"Maybe I could help you move the dresser before I go?" I proposed half-heartedly. Frankly, I doubted even the two of us combined had a snowball's chance in hell of budging the thing even an inch or two, but as a woman with a coffee addiction who'd been short-changed in the bladder department, I couldn't help but sympathize with anyone facing a lack of facilities for any length of time.

"Nah, I'll make do with the powder room downstairs until Kane gets back." She waved off my lackluster offer. "Assuming he gets back."

"So which way did he go?" I asked, pointedly ignoring the cryptic remark she tagged on at the end.

"Good heavens, Maxine! For a relatively intelligent woman, you ask some dumb questions. Which way do you think he went?"

"Well, let's see…" The plan, as I understood it, was for the Hellhound Grim Reaper to confront the Guardian of the Gates of Hell in order to rescue the Zombie King. "I'm going to go out on a limb and guess south?"

I knew I was right when Granny-Apple-Head

amped up her rocking and stomped her orthopedic shoe on the plank floor while launching into an impromptu version of "Highway to Hell."

Don't even attempt the visual. Trust me.

"Well, let's just say you might want to lose that jacket where you're going," she chortled breathlessly, apparently finding heavy metal a bit too strenuous at her age.

"Much as I am enjoying this amazing musical interlude...or not...sadly I've forgotten my handy dandy compass for the directionally challenged. Do you think maybe you could at least point me in the right direction?" I tried to appear casual, as though I had all the time in the world. The grinding sound issuing forth from my molars and the incessant tapping of my foot may have given me away, however.

As we have already established, patience is not one of my virtues.

Granny-Apple-Head choked to a halt just before the chorus, and heaved a deep sigh. She dropped her needles into her lap—yes, they continued to clack away.

Need I reiterate how totally creepy that is?

Then she narrowed her eyes in my direction.

"Well, of course I could point you in the right direction, Maxine, but maybe you should just trip up the steps and have some cookies and gin and wait it out. Are you sure traipsing along after Kane is the best decision?"

I thought about that for a moment. Clearly, the Grim Reaper had not intended for me to tag along. I mean, nothing says *park your ass and wait here* like barricading a girl in the bathroom. Still, I couldn't help thinking it was a mistake for him to leave me behind. Surely, I could be of some help even if bitchy was the only real superpower I was sure I possessed.

"We both know I've made worse. I realize Kane's gotten some crazy idea in his head that seeing him shift is going to change my opinion of him, but I've already seen him and I'm still here, aren't I? Besides, he dragged me into this so if something goes wrong, I am not responsible." Of course, if everything went well, I intended to take full credit and attribute the outcome to my brilliant awesomeness.

"Morgan Kane is a big boy, and he's fully capable of taking care of himself, Maxine. Besides, you don't even like Buddy."

"Well, that may be true, but don't forget his pesky little supernatural superpower. There's that whole saving the world from the Zombie Apocalypse angle to consider."

"Yes, but as I understand it, you agreed to help Kane get him out before you even knew about his potential to create chaos and destruction."

Okay, so maybe Buddy wasn't my favorite person. Maybe I'd had fantasies of giving him a high five...in the face...with a rock. Maybe he didn't deserve the benefit of my doubt. Then again, maybe even before I knew he was the potential bringer of doom, I began to understand that maybe he was just a mixed-up kid who was trying to fit in and find a way to be happy. Maybe, being someone who had some experience with bad decisions and knee-jerk reactions, I even saw a bit of myself not so long ago.

Don't get excited, the similarity is hardly worth mentioning, but there it is.

This new self-awareness crap was really starting to get on my last nerve.

"Are you going to tell me which way to go or just let me wander the afterlife aimlessly?"

"While that might be fun, since I can't dissuade you, the Reaper went that way." She pointed back the way we'd come, settled herself comfortably in her chair, and picked up her needles. Swell. It appeared I was going to have to take my lively mortal energy back through the crowd of sightless, groping souls the Grim Reaper and I had encountered on the way in.

Did I mention they have no eyes?

Yeah, that. And this time I wouldn't have the benefit of Kane's swirling aura of death to trump my bright, shiny glow of life. I closed my eyes and shivered. I had no idea how far their little enclave extended, and the Lost were going to be all over me like a bad rash because I'm, you know, alive which makes them *lurve* me. Fun times.

"You wouldn't happen to own a stun gun, would you?" I groaned, a feeling of dread creeping up my spine as I eyed the milling crowd down the street.

"Hardly," she replied dryly as I offered her a listless wave and started slowly in the direction of the leeches. "Look, Maxine, you do whatever you want. It's pretty clear you're going to anyway. But here's a couple pieces of jerky for you to chew on along the way. First of all, Morgan Kane feels something for you beyond professional courtesy. If Cerberus picks up on it, it makes you someone who can be used against him, just like Alia."

Alia was Morgan's sister whom Cerberus had taken hostage in the hopes of forcing Kane to kowtow to his self-assumed leadership of the Hellhound population. An attempted rescue was the cause of Kane's previously disfiguring scars. Alia had managed to slip away and take refuge at the Timekeeper's where I found her on my first official retrieval mission. She'd been a baby Hellhound at the time, and even as a confirmed cat person, I'd gotten rather attached. So much so, that after I managed to get her out, I was honestly disappointed to find I hadn't acquired a puppy.

Wait a minute...Granny-Apple-Head thought Kane felt something for me?

"Did he, uh, say anything about me that makes you think so?" I asked, keeping my tone deliberately casual. The Timekeeper rolled her eyes. No small feat as they were the size of raisins and buried in the folds of her wrinkled face. I think she may have raised her brows as well, but frankly, it was next to impossible to tell.

"Who am I, an advice columnist? Seriously Maxine, figure your relationships out for yourself. I have enough on my plate keeping the fabric of time free of tangles and knots. I don't have the energy or brain cells left over to play matchmaker or direct people's love lives. Not my job."

"Fine, be that way," I sniffed. Truthfully, there was absolutely nothing about her that reminded me of an advice columnist, but I figured discretion was the better part of self-preservation so I kept my thoughts to myself. "But even if you're right, both Alia and I skillfully managed to outsmart Cerberus' sulfur spewing butt once, and there's no reason to think I can't do it again should the need arise."

"I'm thinking you probably had a short streak of dumb luck. On the other hand, Harvey does adore his leather so maybe you can at least distract him if needed." Her beady little eyes examined me from head to toe. "Double points if he's an ass man. Nice choice, dear."

"Thanks, I think." Honestly, Granny-Apple-Head noticing my ass awesomeness ranked right up there with my father noticing on the crawly scale, but at least she finally appeared to be leaning toward instruction rather than obstruction. "So are you going to help me or what? At this rate, I'll never catch up to Kane."

The Timekeeper set her knitting on the chair beside her, and rose to her feet. Standing at the top of the porch steps and looking down at me where I stood fidgeting at the bottom, she suddenly seemed a lot more menacing than she had before. She planted her hands on her ample hips, causing her gray floral housedress to ride up, giving me an unwanted glimpse of the rolled down tops of her garter-less stockings and her doughy knees. It was not pretty.

"Let me ask you something, Maxine. Do you have feelings for Morgan Kane? Besides unbridled lust?"

"I beg your pardon?"

"Let's face it, just between us girls, Morgan Kane is chocolate covered bacon on a stick. I may be old, dear, but I'm still a woman, and I'm not blind despite the size of my peepers. Not much I can do about it anymore, but I still like to look, if you catch my drift."

"Um, eww?"

The Timekeeper—who was, I don't know, a million years old—had the hots for the Grim Reaper?

"Get your mind out of the gutter, Maxine. I've known Kane since he was a boy, and I don't think of him that way, even if I hadn't given up dessert centuries ago. But I do enjoy his company, and you have to admit, he *is* rather pretty."

Given my unnatural preoccupation with his shoulders and posterior, I couldn't argue with her, and she took my silence for acquiescence.

"The bottom line is, if I help you it's going to piss him off and maybe put the kibosh to his occasional visits, which are one of the few things in this endless existence I look forward to. I'm going to need your assurance he means more to you than a single serving of chocolate lava cake with hot fudge sauce and whipped cream."

"C'mon," I hedged with a grin while shifting my weight from one foot to the other. "You have to admit a helping of chocolate lava cake with hot fudge sauce and whipped cream is pretty awesome." Her lips didn't even twitch, and she simply continued to stare at me with a stern expression from those dark holes nearly buried under her protruding brow.

I sighed. This wasn't just another one of those awkward moments when someone fails to understand my amazing sense of humor.

Hard as it is to believe, it really does happen.

No, this was one of those awkward moments when I had to carefully examine my heart, admit the truth to myself, admit it to the Timekeeper, and—Oh, Holy Night—admit it out loud.

"Fine. While I do not deny the absolute appeal of chocolate lava cake with hot fudge sauce and whipped cream, I will admit the Grim Reaper surpasses even that, and ranks right up there in terms of necessity to my happiness with coffee and jelly doughnuts. Happy, old woman?"

"What is it with you and your preoccupation with food, Retriever? But, yes, your answer is satisfactory. Follow me." She turned, yanked the wooden screen door open, and disappeared into the house.

I hoofed it up the steps in pursuit without so much as a stumble. However, I had no time to revel in my newfound ability to scale elevations unscathed because, dang! That old woman was quick. By the time I burst into the vestibule of the cottage, she was disappearing through another doorway about halfway down the hall. I leapt forward and grabbed for the sleeve of her gray patterned housedress.

"Hey, wait a minute. You're going the wrong way."

"Not at all, dear." She winked with a sly smile. She descended a flight of stairs, swallowed up by the darkness as her voice floated up behind her. "I know a shortcut."

I pinched the bridge of my nose between my thumb and forefinger and paused for a moment to consider whether I had perhaps lost my mind at last. Not so long ago I'd simply been your average bitter divorcée who didn't do change, denying I was still hung up on my ex, and unwilling to admit the divorce had been mostly my fault in the first place. Now here I was with a supernatural sideline, killing time in the afterlife by contemplating a shortcut to Hell, and admitting to feelings for the Grim Reaper, while deluding myself he needed my help in securing the release of the Zombie King? Denise had a lot of nerve to imply I was incapable of change.

I knew I could just sit here and wait as I'd been told, but Morgan Kane made my heart skip a beat, made my bones turn to butter, and made my girly bits quiver. The man had seen me at my worst—who am I kidding, the man had met me at my worst—and he hadn't run away screaming yet. I couldn't help feeling he was the guy. The guy I thought I'd never find again, the guy who really saw me, who actually got me. And who cared about me anyway. I didn't want something to happen to him before I had the chance to find out. The bottom line is if you always do what you've always done you'll always get what you've always had. Polyester golf pants might be safer, they might be saner, but no matter how hard I try, they will never do it for me. Did that make me crazy?

And just for the record, when I ask for your opinion, I don't really want your opinion. I want you to repeat my opinion back to me in a different voice.

"Maxine?" Granny's voice wafted up from the darkness.

I sucked in a deep breath and blew it out again, then put my foot on the first step. What exactly was my plan, again? Oh, that's right. I didn't have one.

Of course, as we have previously established, that'd never stopped me before.

"Coming."

Chapter 15

"In case you hadn't noticed, coordination and I have never been properly introduced. Some light would not be unwelcome," I shouted down the steps as I felt blindly for the wall and slowly descended into the darkness of Granny-Apple-Head's musty basement.

"Haven't you ever heard of energy conservation? You really are high maintenance, Maxine," Granny grumbled as I heard a faint click and the stairwell flooded with light. High maintenance? Me? Hell, I should introduce her to Denise.

I reached the bottom unscathed—*go me*—stepped down onto the packed dirt floor, and took a look around. The stone-walled basement was unremarkable, and reminded me of every other cellar I'd ever seen beneath an older home. Dusty wooden shelves lined the walls, filled with jars whose contents I refused to examine too closely, and tools that clearly hadn't been used in ages. Thick cobwebs clogged the corners and dangled from the rafters. As I moved toward the doorway at the back, I kept my eyes open for any stray eight-legged bastards that might have ideas of avenging their kinsman whom I'd stomped into oblivion at my place earlier in the day.

Hey, it could happen.

I would like to say I was shocked speechless as I stepped through the doorway and got a good gander at

Granny's set-up. But honestly, my WTF meter had given up the ghost ages ago, and we all know I'm rarely if ever speechless.

"Geeks and nerds everywhere would be proud," I sniggered as Granny flitted from panel to panel and dial to dial. Okay, maybe flitted is a bit misleading. Lumbered might be the appropriate term. Lights flashed, screens flickered, sensors beeped, and the Timekeeper's tiny raisin eyes took on a maniacal gleam. I freely admit I was having second thoughts about this shortcut of hers.

"So are you planning to *beam* me to Hell?"

"Don't be ridiculous, Maxine. We don't use sci-fi technology over here. Don't need it. However, I do love my cable, and it's almost time for my favorite show. If you get back in time, we can watch Montel together." With a final, triumphant wheeze, she slapped her hand down on a big red button and a thirty-two-inch flat-screen on the wall sparked to life.

"Is Montel back?" I thought that show was cancelled years ago.

"Given the distance between dimensions..." She waddled over to a raggedy recliner positioned in front of the television and dropped her sizable bulk into it with a relieved grunt. "Afterlife cable operates on a delay. I do love my talk shows, but what I'm really waiting for is the new season of that show where everyone runs around in revealing beachwear. The Hoff...what a hottie!" She licked her index finger and touched it to her hip while making a sizzling sound. I reminded myself she probably didn't get out much.

"Yeah, and he sings, too. The guy is the total package, right? Soooo about that shortcut..." I prodded.

My eyes darted around for anything resembling a door, seeing nothing except the way I'd come in.

"Oh, right. The shortcut." She yanked on a lever on the side of the chair and a footrest popped up under her puffy ankles just as the studio audience went wild with hoots and hollers and the host bounded onto the screen. In living color. After the hours already spent in the monochromatic world of the afterlife, it damn near blinded me, and I squeezed my eyes shut automatically. "Over there in the corner under the manhole cover."

Prying my eyes open, I shuffled over to the corner and stooped down to gauge the weight of the iron disc. I rose to my feet, flexed, stretched, and dug in my pocket for a couple of those magic beans and popped them into my pie hole. Thus fortified with chocolate and caffeine, I braced my hands against the rim and put my back into it. I crunched, I swallowed, I moaned, I groaned. The moan was in total appreciation for the awesomeness of Kane's gift. The groan was directly related to the screaming pain shooting up my spine that I'm pretty sure indicated a herniated disc.

"Don't hurt yourself. It's heavy, dear."

"You don't say," I gasped, desperately sucking air between my teeth and wondering if my Retriever job description had a workman's compensation clause. Somehow, I doubted it. Hopefully my health insurance covered chiropractic adjustments. Or spine transplants. "Thanks for the warning."

Using my hands, I painfully crawled up the wall to a standing position and was relieved to discover my back loosened after a painful spasm or two, and my legs would still hold me. Narrowing my eyes, I peered down into the dark hole, knowing just how Alice must have felt when faced with the conundrum of whether or not to follow that damn rabbit. In fact, I was beginning to relate to Alice on a number of levels. Except in my case, Hell, not Wonderland, was waiting at the bottom. And let's face it, on a scale of one to terrifying, Hellhounds and demons trump playing-card soldiers and tea parties all day long. Given the shiny technology in Granny-Apple-Head's TV room, I admit I'd been kind of hoping to find a well-lit staircase under the cover. With bannisters. And anti-skid rubber treads. Or an elevator.

"How deep is this thing?"

"No idea, dear. I've never used it. My voluptuous curves make it a rather tight fit."

"Why didn't Kane use the shortcut?"

"Please, Maxine, have you seen those shoulders?" She tore her gaze away from the screen and glanced in my direction. Apparently, the drool trickling from the corner of my lips gave me away. "Yeah, I thought you had. He doesn't fit either. Anyway, he prefers to take the long way. He enjoys the exercise. You, clearly, not so much."

"I'm sure I should be insulted on many levels, but frankly I've got bigger fish to fry at the moment." Fighting panic, I lowered myself back to the floor and perched on the perimeter of the opening with my feet dangling over the edge. "So I just...uh...drop into this hole, free fall an undetermined distance for an unknown period of time, and end up... where?"

"From what I understand, you should land just this side of the river Styx," she replied while placidly crunching a handful of tortilla chips.

No, I don't know where she pulled them from, and

that, combined with their unappetizing putty color, kept my junk food craving in check.

"From what you understand? You mean you don't even know?" I screeched. Granny whooped as one potential baby daddy grabbed a chair and cracked it over the back of another. The audience went wild as the burly bouncers leapt into camera range and elbowed their way into the fray to separate the combatants. While chaos ensued on the screen, the Timekeeper went all exorcist impersonator and rotated her head a hundred and eighty degrees to stare at me. It was creepy, but at least she stopped short of spewing pea soup.

We have already established it's not my color.

"Some things must simply be taken on faith, dear. Now, after you land, just wait for Kane to arrive. He's got a pretty good head start so it shouldn't take long. And Max? You might want to reconsider before you drop your ass down that hole. Kane has bigger concerns than your seeing him shift."

Well, gee whiz, didn't that sound all warm and fuzzy? Every word out of Granny-Apple-Head's mouth increased my excitement about my impending trip south. But seriously, what could the Grim Reaper possibly be worried about? In my experience, he'd always been kind, and funny, and thoughtful. Well, except for that pesky little barricading me in the bathroom incident. And the crack about me smelling like a new truck. So maybe when he was running around on all fours he peed on trees or something? Disturbing, but not a deal breaker. I mean, if I wanted to be accepted warts and all, it seemed only fair I was willing to do the same for him, right?

"Okay, let's see if I have this straight. Jump down the hole, pray I don't kill myself, hunker down and wait for Morgan, pray I don't kill myself. That sound about right?" I rubbed my damp palms on my thighs. Surprisingly, leather did not possess the same absorptive properties as denim. Hopefully the breeze on the way down would evaporate the puddles. Well, either that or maybe the moisture would lubricate the passageway should I encounter a particularly tight spot.

"I think that's everything. Just make sure you wait for the Reaper and don't go traipsing off on your own. That's the most important thing."

Frankly, not killing myself was my top priority, but that's just me.

"Um, okay then…here I go." I scooted closer to the edge and bit my lip, shooting a furtive look at Granny and half hoping she had a few more kernels of wisdom to impart.

"Have fun, dear." She turned her attention, and her freaky head, back to the chaos on the screen and shoved another handful of gray chips in her mouth, chomping happily, and effectively dismissing me.

All righty then. I was pretty sure fun wasn't on the menu, but it was nice of her to send me off on an optimistic note.

Why was I doing this again?

Oh yeah, broad shoulders, great ass, promise of a date, Zombie King, saving the world. Check. I took a deep breath, swallowed a scream, and dropped into nothingness.

Which lasted about ten seconds before my feet hit a solid surface and I landed like a ton of bricks, smack on my tailbone.

Yes, it hurt like hell.

I continued my southerly journey in a spiraling downward slide that reminded me of the Drop of Doom at Feel the Wave Waterpark, minus the water. And the middle-aged men parading around in manties. Trust me, even working your eyes over with a cheese grater doesn't erase that image.

Remember when I said I was afraid of heights?

Perhaps this would be a good time to clarify. It's not the actual heights that bother me as much as the falling. Okay, maybe not the falling itself which, let's be honest, is relatively painless. The real problem is that sudden stop at the bottom. I always suspected it would be a real bitch. I discovered I was absolutely right, when instead of a gently lapping pool of chlorine scented, kiddie pee-warmed water, this particular Drop of Doom spit me out flat on my back into a clearing of hard-packed earth, littered with very large rocks. Well, at least it wasn't gray.

Um...freakin' ouch.

I probably could have lounged there for hours staring at the swirling red sky and determining whether I was dead or alive with my mother's fugly necklace scalding a brand into my chest indicating a portal was nearby, except for two things. First, my mother's fugly necklace was scalding a brand into my chest indicating a portal was nearby, and second, I detected a low growl which sounded much too close for comfort emanating from the trees surrounding the clearing. Not comfort was currently a possibility on any level, but as Hell was a whole new travel destination, and I hadn't thought to check the brochure, I had no idea who or what I might run into while waiting for the Grim

Reaper to saunter by on his nature walk.

Keeping my attention firmly fixed on the trees, I dragged myself backwards to the rock face from which I'd been ejected, and feeling like twelve miles of bad road, clawed my way to my feet. Then I cleverly pressed my back to the cliff to ensure nothing could sneak up behind me. Okay, maybe at the moment, it was less about intelligent strategy and more about avoiding the supine shuffle. Being flat on one's back does put a girl at such a disadvantage.

The low growls increased in volume, and the bushes near the edge of the clearing rustled ominously. Whoever or whatever was out there was getting closer. I sucked in a shaky breath, gasping as a sharp, burning pain in my side hinted at a well-bruised rib at the very least. Yes, clearly I was still discovering my supernatural superhero abilities.

It's all about trial and error, people.

Still, I was pretty sure Wonder Woman never had to deal with any of this crap. With shaking fingers, I tugged my fugly necklace out of my shirt to prevent toasted ta-tas, and quickly zipped up my jacket.

As I continued to stare and shake, a long black snout topped by two intense red eyes broke from the cover of the underbrush, and a shaggy, black wolf-like creature the size of a small pony slinked across the clearing in my direction. I slowly released the breath I hadn't even realized I was holding and straightened, carefully moving away from the wall.

"Holy Mother of Pearl, Kane! You scared the bejesus out of me."

The animal offered no hint of recognition and simply continued its stealthy approach. I swallowed a brief flash of terror. He was still in there somewhere, right? I mean, he'd found and rescued me in his animal form once, so he had to be capable of rational thought. Sure, I expected him to be pissed I was here, but he wouldn't tear my throat out at this stage of our relationship, would he? Of course, he very well might want to frighten a decade off my life if he thought it would teach me a lesson.

Refusing to give him the upper hand, I leaned back against the wall crossing one ankle over the other and shoving my hands in my pockets, assuming the most nonchalant pose I could manage given my terror, multiple bruises, and possible broken bones. The Hellhound wasn't nearly as large as I remembered, though granted I hadn't exactly been lucid when I'd last encountered him. The animal was within a foot of me when his snout came up and he swung his furry head from side to side as he scented the air before resuming his advance. Suddenly he lunged forward, rising up on his hindquarters and planting a softball-sized paw against each of my shoulders, pinning me to the wall. His hot, moist breath fanned my face and ruffled my hair. It smelled like ass. Not that I make a habit of sniffing ass for comparison, but there was nothing wrong with my imagination.

"Morgan, I have two words for you. Oral hygiene. Now be a good boy and get down. I realize you are simultaneously impressed and annoyed at my awesome escape skills, but I'm here now so what say you shift back so we can talk about it?"

As though I hadn't spoken, the animal simply continued to stare. Wait a minute, hadn't Morgan's eyes been their usual appealing green even when he'd been in Hellhound form? Oh, damn, they had! And this furry monster had red eyes. I had a heartbeat and a half to realize I might be in trouble before he buried his nose in my neck and then…

"You scurvy bastard! Stop humping my freakin' leg before I plant my knee right in your Cap'n Crunchballs!"

Chapter 16

I suppose this romantic little interlude may have continued indefinitely, if a tree limb hadn't come out of nowhere and caught the rutting hound right in the back of the skull. His head came up with a snarl, and he bared a mouthful of teeth dripping with saliva and a few other things I didn't care to examine too closely.

May I remind you of his desperate need for oral hygiene?

Seconds later, he was torn away from me by the scruff of his neck and flung across the clearing. He bounced off a tree with pained yelp and rolled to his feet, sides heaving. Shaking his head as though to clear it, he aimed a malevolent glare in my direction, and slinked off into the woods.

"What in the hell are you doing here?" roared Morgan Kane who stood not two feet away with his hands fisted at his sides and his nostrils flared like an enraged bull. He wasn't nearly as impressed with my awesome escape skills as I'd hoped. In fact, I'm pretty sure he wasn't even a tiny bit happy to see me. Oh well, at least I didn't have to worry about him wanting to hump my leg, or any other part of me, any time soon.

Can we spell peeved, boys and girls?

"You don't have to shout. I'm standing right here," I snapped, planting my fists on my hips and stepping toward him with an arrogant toss of my head that was purely for show. Seeing his flushed face, I began to have second thoughts about leaving the cozy confines of Granny-Apple-Head's water closet. It suddenly dawned on me that he was six and a half feet of solidly muscled Hellhound Grim Reaper, and he was royally pissed. At me. And we were alone. In Hell. I'd just seen him toss a three-hundred pound animal ten feet in the air. With one hand. Let's face it, he could snap me like a twig should he feel so inclined. I wondered if I would ever reach a point in my life where I didn't end up in a situation preceded by the conviction that it seemed like a good idea at the time.

"Do you have any idea what could have happened to you if I didn't come along when I did?" He grabbed my shoulders, his fingers biting painfully into my flesh, and shook me to emphasize every word. "Do you?"

"Well, clearly I would have had to trash my awesome new leather pants," I choked out. "Because, you know…ewwww."

Whatever he'd been about to say next seemed to stick in his throat as he held me at arm's length and regarded me with an incredulous expression.

"You're pushing it, Logan," he growled at last, loosening his grip but pulling me closer. "Have you ever considered using a glue stick instead of a lipstick every once in a while? No? You should. I had a perfectly good reason, several in fact, for not bringing you along. Was it really so difficult to accept I might know something you didn't, and just do as I asked?"

The more he talked, the more certain I became I was about to rock my very first assault charge. I wondered if it could be counted against me in the real world. Of course, I probably shouldn't take the chance.

A life in prison just doesn't work for me on a number of levels. I'm pretty sure the coffee sucks, the doughnuts are stale, and while Bodacious Bertha in cell block C is undoubtedly a lovely person underneath that beard and all those tattoos, I'd rather not spend ten to life as her soul, er…cellmate. Also, like pastel pink and pea soup green, prison orange is not my color.

"Asked?" I sputtered in self-righteous indignation. "I guess I must have missed that part. Or maybe the sound of the big, heavy, immovable object sliding in front of the bathroom door drowned out your polite request. And I don't use lipstick. I prefer vodka lip gloss, thanks."

His eyes narrowed, and he simply stared at me for a moment. Then to my utter astonishment, he pulled me into his arms and rested his chin on my head with a heavy, resigned sigh. I buried my nose in the front of his T-shirt and drew in a deep breath. Ah, the irresistible aroma of jelly doughnuts took the fight right out of me. Between that and the shoulders—and lest I forget, the magnificent ass—exactly how was I expected to resist this guy? I'm only human, after all. Even if he isn't. Just saying.

He pulled back to look down into my face, and I was struck yet again by the sheer perfection of his features even with the faint hint of scarring that remained, and the ragged remnant of that one tattered ear. With an amused expression, he reached out to tuck a strand of my hair behind my ear, and as his fingers brushed my cheek, I felt something warm and wicked swirl in my gut.

"What in the hell am I going to do with you? You shouldn't be here, Logan. There are things here I would have preferred you never see, never know about. As a Retriever you'd have no reason to ever leave the Between. No one can touch you there as long as you stick to your target and your timetable. Here with me, you're fair game. That complicates things."

As in, he wouldn't simply have to worry about getting Buddy out, now he'd have to worry about me, too. Okay, so I freely admit I'd felt angry and betrayed and didn't stop to consider whether having me along could make his mission extra problematic.

What? You have no experience with bad decisions and knee jerk reactions?

"You're right."

"I'm sorry? I thought you just said I was right."

"I did." I sighed, tipping my head back and losing myself in those incredible emerald eyes. "I know this will come as a shock, but occasionally I react before thinking things through. If you're as smart as I give you credit for, you will let that remark slide without comment. I was angry you left me behind, and I…well, let's just say I guess I thought I had something to prove. I really didn't mean to make this difficult. Obviously, I can't go back the way I came, so just point me in the right direction, and I'll hoof it on back and wait for you at Granny's like you, um, *asked*."

"Too late. Your friend Fluffy will have already announced our arrival, so stealth and the element of surprise are out. I'm going to have to do this through official channels. For better or worse, Logan, you're going in with me. Just promise me from here on out, you follow my lead no matter what happens, and you do exactly as I say. Deal?"

"And if I can't?"

"Well, it would sure as hell make things easier, but nothing about you has ever been easy. And just for the record, if you feel you have things to prove to yourself, have at it. But you don't have to prove a damn thing to me."

His statement produced a profound thought.

What? It happens.

For too much of my life, I'd based my self-worth on the opinions of others, or at least those opinions as I perceived them to be. But letting others have that power has taken me right down the road of unhappily-ever-after more than once. And if I ever hoped to be truly happy again, I had to be me, warts and all. I hadn't exactly been on my best behavior since we'd met, and Kane seemed okay with that. Sure, I intended to cooperate. But if his whole plan went south? Well, I couldn't make any guarantees if I came up with a better idea.

"First of all, I'm already in Hell prepared to take on Buddy and his teenage angst. Let's be clear. Fluffy is no friend of mine. Stop gifting me with these losers. Secondly, where are we going on our date? And third, blind obedience is not my forte, but I'll do my best."

"Well, that's more than I thought I'd get." He didn't argue, he didn't demand. One corner of his mouth even curled up as though he would have been disappointed if I'd responded differently. I resisted the urge to stretch up on my toes and press my lips there. Yes, he was drop dead gorgeous. But beyond that, there's something incredibly appealing about a man who isn't trying to change who you are. Now if I could just work up a good fart, I'd be able to conclusively confirm he was my soul mate.

Kane squeezed me gently and stepped back. The sensation of his arms lingered even after he released me. In order to divert attention away from my breathless trembling, I dug in my pocket for some chocolate covered courage.

"Want some?" I generously offered him the bag as I tossed back a handful of beans.

As you may have already guessed, he'd made the top of my short list as evidenced by my willingness to share my drug of choice.

"Man cannot live by coffee and chocolate alone, Logan." He laughed and shook a few into his palm and popped them in his mouth.

"Well, duh, that's why God invented doughnuts." Honestly, I would have thought that was obvious to anyone. "And just for the record, no matter what you thought when you left me behind, I don't have a problem with you being a Hellhound. I must warn you, however, if you ever turn furry and try to hump my leg, I may have to reconsider my opinion."

"There were other reasons for leaving you behind aside from what you might think of my beast, as you'll find out soon enough. And don't worry, Logan." He started walking in the direction he'd thrown my admirer, and I fell in step behind. "When the time comes, I won't be furry, and it won't be your leg."

And didn't that visual make me trip over my own two feet.

Being uber talented, I managed to stay upright, but I was thankful Kane hadn't bothered to glance back to gauge my reaction since I was pretty sure even with my mad ninja skills, I could not have disguised it as an intentional dance move. It turns out Denise had been correct in her assessment of the unpredictability of March weather and the warmth of my jacket. I was sweating like a hooker in church and drenched in several places I can't politely mention, most of which I couldn't honestly attribute to my awesome ensemble.

As we broke through the trees moments later, Kane stopped in front of me so suddenly, that distracted by my lascivious fantasies, I plowed right into his broad and thickly muscled back. This, of course, necessitated yet another balance-restoring ass grab.

What? I was embracing life, remember?

And if the Grim Reaper's gluteus maximus happened to keep getting in the way, who was I to fight fate? I was delighted to discover it hadn't sagged a bit in the past few hours and was just as scrumptiously round and firm as before. Keeping a secure hold on his tempting globes, I peeked around Kane to determine the cause of his abrupt halt. In front of us, beyond a grassy plain, was a wide river, which I assumed to be the river Styx. My fugly necklace was still cooking at a temperature I could feel even through my shirt, though whether it was the river itself or some other nearby portal causing the reaction, I wasn't sure. At any rate, it was comforting to know there was the potential for a quick getaway should Morgan and I become separated and an escape be required. On the banks of the river ahead, a small group of people stood in an orderly line near a short, wooden pier while a large number of others wandered aimlessly along the shore as far as the eye could see.

"Who are they?" I whispered, though there was no one else close enough to hear.

"The souls of the damned. The ones waiting for the

ferry can pay. The others are doomed to wander the shore for a hundred years before they can cross over."

"Well, I suppose there are worse things than having to delay your arrival in Hell, right? What about us? I should tell you right up front, I didn't bring my purse, and I'm not much of a swimmer. I am, however, a heck of a doggie-paddler."

"No worries." He shoved a hand into the pocket of his jeans and withdrew a collection of small irregularly shaped coins. "I never cross the veil without some viaticum just in case."

"Some what?"

"*Viaticum*. It's a Latin term referring to a provision for a journey. It's also popularly known as Charon's *obol*. Considering your extensive familiarity with epidemiology, Zombie research, and other relatively useless information, I'm surprised you don't know that, Logan. You want to cross the river, you've got to pay the piper, or in this case, the ferryman. In ancient times, the dead were traditionally buried with small coins, and in some regions, the tradition continued right up into the nineteenth century. Eventually it died out, no pun intended, and that's why you see so many souls left to wander. They can't pay the fare."

"What about the ones waiting in line? Some must still follow the custom?"

"Not deliberately, but you've heard the saying you can't take it with you? Some people are greedy enough to try." He shrugged. Wide shoulders, big muscles.

Yeah, yeah we've already established I noticed. Every time.

"So we're going to go down there and get in line for the boat to…" I squinted in disbelief as the far shore came into focus.

Yeah, I'd always thought the place was called Hell too, but the giant billboard flashing a blinding sequence of lights on the opposite side of the river said otherwise.

Apparently, the basement of the afterlife was known in these parts as Sin City South. Catchy, right? Beyond the billboard stretched a conglomeration of garishly lit buildings gaudy enough to rival the Vegas strip. Not a pile of smoking brimstone or a single lake of fire anywhere in sight. I suppose at this point, it should not have come as a surprise.

"You have *got* to be kidding!"

Kane reached back and pried my resisting fingers away from his ass. Then he pulled me around in front of him. Cupping my jaw, he buried his fingers in my hair and tilted my face up to his. His lips brushed over mine like a spring breeze, light, warm, and filled with promise.

He lifted his mouth from mine, and while I clung to the front of his shirt and tried to remember how to breathe, he stared over my head with narrowed eyes. His voice had an edge to it as he continued. "I've waited a long time for you, Logan, and I'd really hoped to avoid a meet and greet with my family. They don't make the best first impression."

"And I do? Anyway, I've met your sister and she's a lovely girl. In fact, I was even prepared to forgo my deeply ingrained cats-only convictions and take her on as a pet." His brows drew together in a dark frown. "Well, that was before I knew she wasn't actually a homeless dog," I added in a rush.

Wait a second... he'd been waiting for me?

"Alia is good kid who, thankfully, is nothing like our mother." He rested his hand at the small of my back and gave me a gentle shove in the direction of the river. "Whatever happens over there, try not to hold it against me. Just remember, you can't pick your relatives."

Chapter 17

As we descended a small rise and traversed the flat open field of high waving grasses, I spied a boat pulling away from the opposite shore on a slow return trip in our direction. Kane grabbed my hand and began to walk faster, apparently in a hurry to board. The terrain was uneven, sloped toward the water, and the grass came nearly to my knees. It seemed almost alive the way it kept tangling around my feet and causing me to stumble. Of course, considering our location, it wasn't outside the realm of possibility that it actually was.

"Sheesh, could you maybe slow down? Short person, stumpy legs back here, remember?" I panted, clinging desperately to his hand while being dragged along. "What's the rush? I don't know about you, but I'm not in any great hurry to cross the river to Hell, er...Sin City South."

"Sorry." He immediately shortened his stride, allowing me to catch up. I released his hand and bent double, gripping my knees and sucking in air. "Since my original plan to sneak in and steal Buddy hit the skids the moment you arrived and made nice with Fluffy, I'm going to have to go through official channels to get him out. The sooner I do that, the sooner we can get out of here."

"I'm totally on board with the getting out of here part." I straightened and stretched. Then I drew in a deep breath and reached for his hand as if it was the most natural thing in the world. "Who do we have to petition to get Buddy released? And please don't tell me it's your bigger, nastier cousin, because I suspect he won't be especially receptive to the idea."

"Wayne Newton." His fingers curled around mine, and he tugged me forward, then wrapped an arm around my shoulders and tucked me into his side as we continued walking toward the pier at a more sedate pace in deference to my vertically challenged stature and well-known lack of coordination.

"Wayne Newton is in Hell? Well, shoot! I didn't even know he died." I looked up at him in confusion.

"He didn't." He flashed a brief smile that didn't linger as he kept his attention firmly fixed on our destination. "But illusion is everything here, and it's the second Sunday in March. Vegas Week."

"Gee, I wish you'd mentioned it sooner. Vegas Week in Hell and me without a G-string to call my own." I decided I wouldn't even ask.

See? I can show restraint.

Though it doesn't happen often, occasionally I make an executive decision to play ostrich. Besides, deep down I knew ignorance was a temporary reprieve. No matter what I did, eventually I was going to get the whole story anyway.

"Well, I've still got a few connections. If you play your cards right, maybe we can rustle you up some pasties with tassels," he shot back. "And as pleasantly distracting as I find the idea of you prancing around in a G-string, the boat's almost here. We need to step on it."

We attached ourselves to the end of the line just as the ferry chugged into the boat slip alongside the pier.

The excitement in the waiting crowd was palpable. I wondered why anyone would giddily anticipate a damned eternity filled with every sin imaginable, then realized the fact that these souls were here in the first place was its own answer. Mostly. As the narrow gangplank was lowered, the condemned souls surged forward, laughing, chattering, and jostling for position. Clenching my teeth, I secured my fingers in the belt loop of Kane's jeans and let myself be caught up in the wave.

The line moved quickly and before I knew it we were front and center. Kane shoved a hand in his pocket for the viaticum that would guarantee us a ride. The action tugged his jeans down just low enough to afford me a tantalizing glimpse of his rock hard abs, and one side of the nameless cord of muscle guaranteed to make smart girls stupid that traced along his hip and disappeared into his waistband. My mouth went dry. Apparently, even the prospect of petitioning Wayne Newton for the Zombie King's release during Vegas Week in Sin City South was insufficient distraction when it came to my contemplation of the Grim Reaper's physique.

Don't judge me.

"Charon." Morgan greeted the boatman in a neutral tone.

"Hey, Morgan, been a while. Your mother expecting you?"

"She wasn't. Probably knows I'm coming by now, though." Kane's voice was drier than the Mojave and there was a curious tension to his posture. Thinking perhaps the Dread Captain Charon was the reason, I risked a peek up at the boat pilot who was hanging over the side as the Grim Reaper stretched an arm over my head to pay the fare. Okay, I freely admit I was nervously anticipating the stereotypical Charon of myth and legend. Perhaps a skeletal old man clad in foul rags with haggard cheeks and an unkempt beard or maybe even Michelangelo's Last Judgment interpretation of a chunky muscular demon with sharp teeth, pointed ears, and an oar at the ready to beat the crap out of any soul foolish enough to tarry and screw with his schedule. What I was not expecting was an overweight man in white twill pants, a blue polo shirt with matching sneakers, and a jaunty nautical cap.

"Seriously? Let me guess…a hold out from Sixties Sitcom Week? Will we be sharing a cabin with the redhead and the brunette?"

"Yes, no, and behave." Kane's hot breath tickled my ear, and I shivered before he straightened and gripped my upper arm to steady me as I awkwardly navigated the narrow plank from the dock to the deck. "Charon's beef has always been that no matter what week Satan celebrates, the character opportunities for boat captains are limited, so he just paddles to his own current regardless of what's happening on the mainland." Feeling the heat of his palm like a brand even through my clothes, I once again wondered if Hellhounds ran a naturally hotter basal body temperature than humans. I do know the closer Kane was, the hotter I felt.

Though I wasn't ordinarily prone to claustrophobia, something about being crammed like a metal head in a mosh pit with a gang of condemned souls on a bobbing barge to damnation made my knees wobbly and my stomach churn. As if sensing my distress, Kane shouldered us a path through the tightly packed crowd and across the rocking deck to the rail. Breathing required less effort once we were facing out over the water, and I probably would have felt moderately less anxious, too, if not for two things— Kane's hard body pressed against my back and the crowd gathering on the far shore with diaphanous black shadows that looked like big creepy worms cavorting around them. If the Seekers were present among the waiting throng, I was fairly certain I knew the identity of the giant in black leather standing with the main group. At his side, front and center, stood a tall, broad shouldered man wearing what appeared to be a bedazzled tuxedo on his back and a shapely blonde showgirl on his arm.

"So," I drawled in what was intended to be a casual tone but somehow came out all shaky and breathless. Yeah, that. "Does the welcoming committee always gather to greet the new arrivals?"

"Nope." His arms came around me from behind, pulling me back against him as the boat lurched forward. "All that lovin' is just for us."

"Wucking fonderful." I shivered and his arms tightened. Sure, I was all about rescuing Buddy and saving the world, but somehow I'd managed to conveniently overlook the fact that I might run into anyone unsavory in the course of the mission. Sometimes my own worst enemy is the empty space right between my ears. "So what's the plan?"

"The plan *was* for me to sneak in and snatch Buddy from under my cousin's nose. Your unexpected arrival and subsequent twerking session with Toad kind of put the skids to that."

"Excuse me? I do not twerk. Well, maybe in the privacy of my own home. And okay, there was that one ill-advised demonstration in the Supersave parking lot when Denise dared me. But I did absolutely nothing to encourage that mangy mutt, and I can't help it if that he was overcome by the hotness of my leather attire. While I'll admit, his method of expressing his appreciation left something to be desired—I mean, you know, eww—he probably couldn't help himself, so there's no reason to resort to name-calling."

"I wasn't resorting to anything. Toad *is* his name."

"Oh."

I expected the crossing would take a while. Okay, I *hoped* the crossing would take a while, say a month, but we seemed to be racing toward the opposite shore at lightning speed. I could now clearly see Cerberus' smug expression, though Wayne Newton's face remained unreadable. The smile on the face of the showgirl, however, grew exponentially wider the closer we got.

"So you're saying we don't have a plan? No, wait, you're saying I screwed up the plan. Given my track record, that shouldn't surprise you, but for what it's worth, I'm sorry. I'm working on it, okay?"

Kane turned me in his arms, away from my nervous contemplation of the knot of people waiting on the shore. I tilted my head back and rested my chin on his chest. His broad, muscular chest.

Hey, the situation was not yet so dire that I could overlook the obvious.

He squinted over my head at the welcoming committee, and there was a tense tic doing a sporadic jig in his cheek.

"I originally had no intention of bringing you along at all," he ground out at last through tightly clenched teeth. "I planned to snatch the kid and stash him at the Timekeeper's where no one could touch him, and bring you over afterwards just to get him out. But then I saw you again last night and...well, let's just say I was selfish. This is my fault, not yours, Logan."

Wrapping my arms around his trim waist, I wrinkled my nose and looked up at him. "Well, if that bridesmaid dress didn't scare you into the second Tuesday of next week, maybe it isn't a question of fault, but a matter of fate. However we got here, here we are. Now we just have to decide how we're going to play it."

"I have to admit it was a Herculean feat to overlook that dress." He continued to stare out over the water, but his eyes crinkled in amusement. "Well, there isn't any point in trying to reason with Cerberus. He'll refuse to surrender the kid just for spite. I'm going to have to go over his head, and Satan never grants a petition without getting something in return."

"Satan?" I squeaked. "I'm going to meet Satan?"

"Well, this *is* Hell regardless of what they're calling it at the moment. Don't sweat it. He's bearable as long as he doesn't start singing. He can rock the rhinestones, but the pipes are sadly lacking."

"*Wayne Newton* is Satan?" My childhood Catechism teacher, Sister Mary Eloise, better known among the Sunday school set as Sister Myrtle Elephant, would have kittens if she knew how totally off base she'd been with the whole cloven-hooved, pitchfork packing demon description she'd been selling all these years. My mood improved considerably as I pictured the look on her face if I ever had the opportunity to tell her the truth.

"Of course not, and I doubt Mr. Newton would appreciate the comparison. Still, he is the undisputed King of the Strip. Told you, it's Vegas Week." The Grim Reaper held me steady as the boat bumped up against the pier.

Because we'd moved to the far side of the boat for the crossing, we were the last to disembark, which was fine with me, because I wasn't in any big hurry to, *you know*...meet the Devil. The condemned souls streamed down the gangplank ahead of us. White coated ushers waited to the left of the pier and directed the arriving guests to an idling line of minivans.

Yes, minivans.

The organized chaos was ignored for the most part by the Leader of the Banned and his entourage whose undivided attention appeared to be reserved solely for Kane and me.

Isn't that special?

Our turn to disembark arrived. Morgan jumped to the pier, and then he held out a hand to lead me down the ramp.

"See ya, Morgan," the Skipper impersonator called out, tipping his cap in Kane's direction. The Grim Reaper raised his hand in a careless wave and then steered me in the direction of dry land. As soon as we began moving, the blond showgirl detached herself from Wayne's—er, Satan's—arm, and hurried forward with tiny mincing steps, necessitated no doubt, by a pair of stilettos so high, they put even Denise's most extreme pair on a par with ballet flats. The woman's feathered headpiece and bejeweled boobs bounced rhythmically as she approached. Despite the brevity of her attire, she was wearing so many colors she looked as though she'd been gang banged by a box of crayons. Sometimes you just want to ask people if they own a mirror.

When she was a few feet away, she threw open her arms, and Morgan slowly dropped my hand and stepped forward stiffly to greet her. Okay, so maybe her fashion sense was even more questionable than mine, but wardrobe choices aside, I couldn't deny she was absolutely gorgeous. She had a thick mane of golden blonde hair, sparkling green eyes, and smooth porcelain skin sheathing a figure guaranteed to make men drool. I'll admit, the green-eyed monster tiptoed up behind me and nibbled away at my butt as the woman threw herself at the Grim Reaper, even though it was clear to anyone observing that her excitement far eclipsed Morgan's.

"Darling! It's been far too long," she gushed, wrapping her lily white arms around Kane's neck and pulling his head down to plant a smacking kiss on each cheek. While he didn't resist, neither did he share her enthusiasm. I welcomed a tiny niggle of relief. Okay, so maybe Kane thought I had a pretty head and admittedly appreciated my leather-clad butt, but I was well aware I couldn't compete with this chick on any level of physical attraction, and it did my heart good to see he was not impressed.

The blonde pulled back slightly and fixed her stare on me where I stood quietly behind Kane. Her smile dimmed, and her perfectly manicured brows drew together as her gaze swept up and down my leather-clad form from head to toe. I lifted my chin and stared right back, though I was unable to control the warmth suffusing my cheeks as her expression screamed I'd been assessed and found lacking.

Biotch.

"That is *not* your sister." Kane reached back for my hand and dragged me forward to his side. No small feat since Miss Las Vegas was still wrapped around him like a well-endowed octopus.

"You know very well Alia is away at school. This is Max Logan. She's the new Retriever for the Northeast Region," Kane announced, giving my fingers an encouraging squeeze. "Logan, I'd like you to meet my mother, Celina Kane."

"Holy crap! Your mother is Satan's girlfriend?" Two sets of brows flew toward the swirling red sky.

Oops, did I say that out loud? Open mouth, insert fugly foot. My bad.

"Wife actually." Kane appeared to be in danger of choking on the smile he was fighting to suppress. Don't judge me, he mouthed.

"I'm, uh, so sorry," I stammered, holding out a hand. "I was just surprised. Occasionally my mouth operates completely independently from my brain. Morgan never mentioned your, ah, marriage."

Staring me down with an expression I was certain she reserved for particularly offensive insects, she touched her hand to mine briefly, and nodded a regal acknowledgment of my apology. Then she stepped away from Kane and turned back toward the knot of people waiting at the end of the pier.

"Come along, dear. As soon as we heard you were coming, Luc reserved you a suite. I'm sure you and your, ah, Retriever will want to freshen up before the show." Her heels clicked a rapid staccato of annoyance as she preceded us to shore. No matter what I thought of her choice in bedmates, I couldn't help but be impressed at her ability to stomp off in those shoes without breaking an ankle.

"We won't be staying that long," Kane said to her retreating back. She seemed not to hear. Or maybe she chose not to hear. Or maybe I'd finally lost my freakin' mind. I mean, c'mon, I was in Hell with the Grim Reaper whose mother was the Bride of Satan, an apparent closet Wayne Newton impersonator. At this point, anything was possible.

"Satan is your father?" I tugged Kane down to my level and hissed in his ear. "Don't you think you could have mentioned that a little sooner?"

"Stepfather. Told you, you can't pick your relatives."

"Oh." So, he wasn't directly descended from the Prince of Darkness. That was a relief, I guess. I suddenly had a new appreciation for Stepmother Gail. As stepparents go, I'd been riding the gravy train. Right then and there, I made up my mind I was going to buy her something really nice when we got back. Maybe a bigger coffee carousel. Though, frankly I doubted there was any gift that could truly express my appreciation for the fact she wasn't evil incarnate.

"Celina killed her first two husbands, one of whom was my father. While he probably deserved it, to be honest I've always harbored a little resentment."

"I can imagine." Of course, the concept fell so far outside my sphere of possibility, I absolutely couldn't, but I was hoping to impress him with my well-developed sense of empathy.

What? Practice makes perfect, right?

"Hence the reason I don't visit often. Well, that and the fact my mother is completely certifiable."

Well, isn't that special?

My palms were sweating so profusely by now my hand would have slipped right out of his if he weren't currently crushing my fingers. It was a tiny bit uncomfortable, but the pain kept me anchored, both to him and to reality. Honestly, I wasn't so sure that second part was a good thing since my current reality consisted of skipping down the Highway to Hell hand in hand with the ass-tastick Grim Reaper whose mother was a psychotic sociopath married to the Root of All Evil cleverly disguised as Mr. Entertainment surrounded by Cerberus and the Seekers. None of whom were particular friends of mine. Throw in the fact I was doing this all this in the name of rescuing a screwed up kid I wasn't even sure I liked, and this was quickly becoming the biggest too-much-shit-not-enough-shovels day I'd ever had.

Chapter 18

My introduction to the Midnight Idol went marginally better than the one to his blushing bride. Perhaps because I'd had a few minutes to gather my wits, or perhaps because he really did bear a striking resemblance to Wayne Newton. Well, with the exception of the glowing red eyes. Still, when Satan took my hand and belted out the refrain from a 1965 ballad, it was difficult to feel all that threatened. Kane's tense stance, however, warned me not to be lulled into a false sense of security by a couple of off key phrases and buckets of charm. Celina had reattached herself to her husband's arm, and the entire length of his left side, and I was sad to note that even the petulant pout didn't detract from the woman's stunning glamour. It should be illegal for bat shit crazy to look so good.

"I assume you know why we're here?" Kane snatched my hand from Satan's and tugged me closer to his side.

"I wouldn't be Wayne Newton if I didn't," Lucifer replied easily. "Of course, there's the pesky little matter of the contract."

"That's right, cousin," Cerberus added his growling voice to the mix. "Or had you forgotten the kid signed on the dotted line?"

Oh great! So now, in addition to the threat of torture, damnation, and imminent death, we had legal issues to contend with. While I might be the reigning Queen of Useless Knowledge on a wide variety of trivial topics, my understanding of contract law and the legal system in general was pretty much nil. I had difficulty absorbing anything that couldn't hold my interest, and frankly, everything related to legalities bored me. Well, except for Judge Julie. I mean, who isn't equally awed and entertained by her impressive grasp and implementation of civil statutes?

I shot a worried glance at Kane. He was nodding sagely while fighting unsuccessfully to keep the corners of his lips from twitching.

"I wouldn't be the Grim Reaper if I didn't know about the contract, Lucif...um, Wayne. However, according to my sources, it was a temporary contract that expired months ago, and the kid's been here against his will ever since. Isn't that right, *Harvey*?"

All heads swiveled in Cerberus', aka Harvey's, direction. The Seekers swirled around their leader protectively as his eyes widened and his smooth, olive complexion mutated to a shade that strongly resembled pea soup green. Huh! It wasn't his color either. Go figure.

"Is this true, Harvey?" the Prince of Darkness asked in a quiet, conversational tone belied by the dark flush creeping up his neck and suffusing his face. Curiously, he resembled Wayne Newton less and less as the tense moments ticked by. "I distinctly recall passing an edict that all contracts entered into with mortals were to be soul-binding and eternal."

"Well, I didn't think that applied to the kid. I mean, after all, he isn't completely mortal, Boss," Cerberus stammered lamely. Beads of perspiration had popped out on his wide forehead, banding together to trickle down his face and drip from the end of his long Roman nose. He didn't appear nearly as attractive as he had the last time we'd met. I guess some people just don't wear desperation well.

"I don't pay you to think, Harv. Let's take this inside," Satan ordered harshly. He laid a hand over Celina's where it rested on his blue satin sequined sleeve, and began to turn away toward the brightly lit strip.

"No," Kane replied just as harshly. "The kid's been through enough. Let's just get this settled here and now."

The Devil turned back slowly and arched a dark brow at the Grim Reaper as Celina put a hand to her lips and giggled inappropriately.

"Excuse me?"

"Look, if we go inside and Logan gets an eyeful of that complimentary all-you-can-eat dessert buffet, this could take all night. You've got a show to do. It'd be a shame to keep your eager audience waiting. Far be it from me to screw with your schedule. So how about we just take the kid and go?"

I knew Kane was using my addiction to all things carbohydrate as an excuse. I wanted to be insulted, but I couldn't. Facts are facts. A complimentary all-you-can-eat dessert buffet? Yeah, he was right. I'd probably set up a tent. Wayne Newton drank me in from head to toe with a heated expression that did nothing to further endear me to his psycho bride.

"Well." Mr. Entertainment leered. "If Ms. Logan is as obsessed with empty calories as you claim, she must have an overactive metabolism to maintain that figure."

Metabolism? *Moi?* I straightened my shoulders, stuck out my cha-chas, and considered whether I should make Satan my new best friend.

Does that make me bad?

"Fine. Let's settle it. Bring the boy," Satan called out, snapping his obscenely ringed fingers in the air.

There was a commotion in the back of the crowd, and then Buddy appeared, looking pathetic, defeated, and much the worse for wear. His clothes were filthy and tattered. One lens of his coke bottle glasses was as crackled as a spider-web and the other was missing entirely. His greasy hair hung lank and limp around his gaunt shoulders and half covered his face. He was hustled to the front of the assembly by two athletic men with smooth, sculpted chests peeking flirtatiously between the lapels of identical white satin suits, topped by silver marabou trimmed capes. A charming retinue of white baby tiger cubs toddled awkwardly in their wake. With a low bow and a synchronized cape flourish, the men, wearing matching smiles, presented Buddy. Then they spun away, taking the tigers with them and leaving the kid standing small and alone in the empty space between the Devil and his guard dog.

"Holy night! Do you know who that is?" I gasped. I'd always wanted to see their show live. The animals, the props, the lights…the magic! Yes, their teeth really were that white. Of course, anyone's smile looks brighter against a good spray tan, but still.

"Do you think maybe we can…?"

"No."

My shoulders slumped. Well, all righty then.

"Who are they when it isn't Vegas Week?"

"You don't want to know."

At the sound of Kane's voice, Buddy picked up his head and squinted around, his eyes widening in shocked recognition as he spied the Grim Reaper and me. A barely perceptible glimmer of hope flared in his eyes, and my heart caved in. Kane was right. Whatever his faults, whatever his powers, at this moment, he was simply a terrified kid, and we were the best shot he had.

Can we spell poor bastard, boys and girls?

"If I may, your Royal Evilness?" I arched a brow in Satan's direction. He raised his chin regally, looked down his nose at me as though assessing whether or not I was being sarcastic—*which, let's be honest, under most circumstances would not have been outside the realm of possibility*—and then nodded shortly. Kane groaned under his breath as I released his hand and stepped forward. Yeah, I doubtless would regret this unwelcome burst of intuitiveness, but I found the silent pleading in Buddy's eyes, combined with Cerberus' leather clad ass squirming in terror and uncertainty, somehow inspiring.

"I think we can all agree whether or not Buddy is mortal is just semantics, Harvey," I began in what I hoped was a confident sounding voice. "Of course, since I've just met him and I can't say for sure, I suppose it's entirely possible Mr. Newton harbors sufficient affection for you in the cockles of his black heart to allow your blatant disregard of his orders to go unpunished."

Although given Satan's furious expression and the flames erupting from his fingertips, coupled with the rank smell of fear emanating from Cerberus, I thought it unlikely. Kane covertly tugged at the back of my jacket, no doubt hoping I'd take the hint and simply shut my mouth. But, subtlety and I have never been friends and I had an ace up my leather sleeve. Cerberus might still find a way to ingratiate himself with Satan, so I decided to put my money on Celina. Hell might hath no fury like a woman scorned—well, unless she's menstruating and hungry, too, in which case you should probably just kill yourself—but, do you know what's even more dangerous? Getting between a crazy bitch and her pups. And if I was wrong? Well, we wouldn't be in any deeper shit than we were already. I hoped.

Hey, everyone has a gift. Rationalization is mine. Tell me this surprises you.

"Is there a point to your tired monologue, Ms. Logan?" Celina inquired in a bored voice. "My Pookie has a matinee at eight, and it's very bad form to keep an audience waiting."

Her thick, heavily mascara-ed lashes tangled like spider's legs as she lowered them and huffed a breath on her ridiculously long acrylic nails before buffing them on the rhinestone strap of her push up bra. I was pretty sure that might do more harm than good, but hey, I'm no cosmetologist so what do I know?

"Actually…" Taking advantage of my momentary fascination with Mrs. Satan's manicure, Kane finally succeeded in hooking his fingers in the hem of my jacket, and yanked me backwards against him. I gave him kudos for the restraint he showed in not simply slapping his palm over my mouth in the process. I also gave myself kudos for not throwing myself into his arms and hiding my face in his chest while pretending I was on a sandy beach with hot cabana boys and endless cocktails. Instead, I kept my attention firmly fixed on Satan and the Sociopath, schooling my features into a friendly and pleasantly expectant expression.

"As I was saying," I continued after tipping my head back and favoring the Grim Reaper with a fierce frown. "I can certainly understand why your husband might tender leniency in Harvey's case. I mean, he *is* the undisputed Guardian of this southern piece of paradise, after all. But frankly, Celina, the depth of *your* capacity for forgiveness astounds me."

"Me?" She blinked at me blankly. "What does Harvey's contract with the Zombie King have to do with me?"

"Oh, I wasn't talking about the contract, I was talking about your children." I paused portentously. Kane's massive chest vibrated against my back as a low rumble of laughter worked its way up into his throat. He barked out a cough to hide it. Seriously, he barked. His grip on my shoulders relaxed, telling me he'd figured out where I was going with this and he wasn't going to interfere. My heart swelled. He trusted me. While I never leave home without a pocketful of crazy, his mother almost certainly had to cart hers around in an eighteen-wheeler. I was counting on the cray-cray, and he knew it. Perceptive doggie.

"I mean, it was bad enough he tore Morgan to shreds, leaving all those horrible scars. Okay, sure they healed, so I can see how you might be willing to overlook it. Of course, his ear will never be the same…"

"What?" Celina hissed as she released her husband's arm and tottered forward on those obscenely high heels to reach over my head and grasp Morgan's chin. He didn't resist as she dug in her nails and wrenched his head to the side for a clear unobstructed view of the mangled ear. "When did this happen? Why didn't you tell me?"

"I'm a big boy, Mother," he replied calmly, capturing her hand and pressing his lips to her fingers. "I hardly need to hide behind your skirts. Well, I mean if you, you know, had skirts."

"I have skirts, dear, but I don't bring them out until Fabulous Fifties Week. I'm all about the crinoline." She turned back to her husband. "Darling, I simply will not stand for that mangy mutt laying his filthy paws on my son."

"Morgan gives as good as he gets, my love," the Dark Lord responded amicably, his Wayne Newton persona now firmly back in place and a faint smile shadowing his lips under the pencil thin mustache. "He doesn't need you to fight his battles for him."

"You're so right, Mr. Newton. Morgan definitely can take care of himself." I smiled coldly at Cerberus, almost feeling sorry for him. Almost. "But poor Alia…I mean…oops, did I say that out loud?"

"Alia?" Celina's voice dropped three octaves and dripped icicles as her stare bored a hole into the middle of Cerberus' forehead. "You dared to lay a finger on my daughter?"

"Well, not so much a finger as a fist if I remember correctly," I offered helpfully, now that I'd gone and—oh, dear—let the dog out of the bag. "And then there was that whole kidnapping episode. Oh, and the leash. Of course, I was only witness to a small part of it. As to what else may have happened while he held her against her will, I guess you'd have to ask Harvey for the gory details."

Celina's posture stiffened ominously, and her

entire body trembled with rage. She raised an arm in front of her and pointed her outstretched index finger at Cerberus like the Ghost of Christmas Past leading Scrooge through the cemetery. The Seekers' agitation escalated to such a degree it was impossible to differentiate one from the other until, as a single great black cloud, they zipped away in the direction of the nearest casino. Apparently, their loyalty to Cerberus didn't extend to standing between him and Celina. Abandoned by his minions, all remaining color left the Guardian's face, and a dark stain appeared in the crotch of his leathers and slowly spread. Well, what do you know? Silly me, I'd assumed he was housebroken.

"You. Will. Pay." It was Celina's perfect rosebud mouth which moved, but it released a frightening and unrecognizable voice from some deep, dark place inside her.

"Oh dear, now you've done it," the Devil drawled mildly and without a trace of regret. "You've opened the box and let the crazy out." Cerberus glanced around wildly, and after a moment of apparent indecision, turned tail and took off in the direction of Main Street, Sin City South.

"Luc," Celina whined in a petulant little girl voice. "Some help, please? I can't possibly hunt in these shoes."

Hmm, let's see, was that personality number three or four?

"As you wish, my love." Satan waved his hand, and the air around his wife shimmered like the heat rising off an Arizona highway in August. When the waves cleared, Celina was rocking a pair of pink spandex leggings with a matching sports bra and running shoes. Her blonde hair was secured in a high ponytail with a perky pink bow that bounced jauntily with every movement of her head. I was sad to note pink definitely *was* her color. Naturally. She skipped over to Lucifer like a giddy schoolgirl and planted a big wet one on his cheek as his arm came around her and hugged her against his side.

"I'll be home before the midnight show, darling." She turned her attention to her son. "Sorry, I have to run, but it was lovely to see you, sweetheart. Give Alia my love. Come back and visit us for Eighties Hair Band week...and bring your girlfriend. I like her. She's got moxie." With a wiggling finger wave to us both, she slipped from her husband's embrace and took off at an easy jog in the direction Cerberus had taken. Kane's arms came around me, and I sagged against him, releasing a breath I hadn't even realized I'd been holding.

"I love you, Morgan. But, while I freely acknowledge my family can be the happiest group of crazies this side of the loony bin, I'm sorry to inform you that your mother is a flipping fruit loop." He spun me around so quickly my eyes crossed. Not an attractive look, I know. Gripping my shoulders hard enough to leave bruises, he leaned down to peer into my face while I concentrated on refocusing his two heads into one beautifully familiar face which was wearing a most peculiar expression.

"What did you say?"

"I, uh...I said your mother is cuckoo...you know, like the handcrafted clocks from the Black Forest in Germany? Oh sure, she's beautiful—I mean I see where you and Alia get your looks—but really, she's a few doughnuts short of a dozen, isn't she? I'm so sorry, Morgan. Then again, the first step toward forgiveness is understanding the other person isn't responsible if she's bat shit crazy, right? Maybe you shouldn't hold your father's murder against her."

I patted the bulge of his biceps sympathetically, as though focusing attention on his mother's mental incapacities might distract him from my own moment of temporary insanity. Forkity, fork, fork, fork! The L word. I'd said the L word! And I was pretty sure it was too late to pass it off as a pop culture reference to the pay channel television drama of the same name. Those lakes of fire must be closer than I thought. Clearly, while I concentrated on tweaking the crazy, those fires insidiously fried my brain. The heat currently scalding my face was proof.

"Logan…" he began, his face softening. My heart pounded painfully. A thick knot formed in my throat, making it impossible to swallow as I realized that while I hadn't meant to say it, I couldn't say I didn't mean it. Oh shit, I so desperately didn't want to hear the *it's not you it's me* speech. Blah, blah, blah…think of you as a sister, blah, blah…we'll always have Sin City South, blah. Nope, not now, not ever, and definitely not in the presence of a much too interested Lucifer and company.

"Hey, Buddy," I called out, tearing myself from Kane's arms and motioning the silent kid over. "C'mon, kid, let's go home."

In less than a heartbeat, he limped in my direction as though he'd spent a lifetime awaiting an invitation, and threw himself into my arms with a relieved sob. Comforting him was somewhat awkward since he topped me by several inches, but I raised up on my toes and gave it my best shot. Finally, with a phlegmy sniffle, he picked up his head and dragged a tattered sleeve across his face.

"No one has ever cared what happened to me. After everything I've done, why do you?"

"Well, I have to admit, I didn't at first. But someone helped me to see things differently." I glanced furtively at Kane who still hadn't taken his eyes off of me. "I realize you're the potential bringer of doom, but now that I've gotten over wanting to strangle you, I see a kid who just wants to be happy. I guess maybe, I even see a little bit of someone I used to be. Don't get excited, the resemblance is hardly worth mentioning. Anyway, I guess everyone deserves a second chance."

"Thank you," he said simply, but the look in his eyes, at least the one behind the missing lens that I could see, said more than those two innocuous words could ever convey.

"Um, Logan?" The words were soft, as deep and smooth as melted chocolate, and spoken so close to my ear that Kane's warm breath heated my cheek like a caress. With one arm still wrapped around Buddy, I squeezed my eyes closed and swallowed hard, bracing myself for the certain rejection sure to be forthcoming as a result of my unguarded confession.

"Kane, can we just forget it? I didn't mean to say it, okay? You know me, always leaping before I look…I'm working on it, really. I mean, I…"

"You didn't mean it?" His voice was no longer soft and no longer caressing my cheek.

"Of course I meant it. I always mean what I say, I just don't always mean to say it. Please note the difference."

"Don't feel too badly, Logan, I already knew."

"You...already knew I loved you?" I choked out, strangled by mortification as Buddy slipped free of my arms and stepped back after a worried glance over my head at the Grim Reaper. Had I really been so transparent? The ass grabbing...it had to have been the ass grabbing that gave me away.

"No, I already knew my mother was bat shit crazy. Why do you think I didn't want you down here with me? Hell, I've got as much baggage as the lost and found at La Guardia."

"You think I don't have baggage? You *have* met me, right? Everyone's got baggage, Kane. I need an entire airplane hangar for mine."

"Well, okay, so we agree everyone's got baggage. I guess it's just a question of who you trust to help you unpack." He narrowed his eyes, taking in both our surroundings and our audience before returning his attention to me and blowing out a breath. "This isn't exactly how I planned this, but are you willing to swap luggage, Logan? Because as long as we're spilling our guts, I guess I should tell you, I love you, too."

Chapter 19

When it comes to Murphy's Law, I am frequently mistaken for the poster child. Case in point. According to Murphy's Eighth Law, if everything seems to be going well, you have obviously overlooked something. In my defense, a declaration of love closely followed by the Grim Reaper's tongue down my throat is enough to make me forget my name, let alone the fact I was standing at the entrance to Hell with the Prince of Darkness observing the entire exchange from mere feet away. I'm not sure how long I might have remained obliviously content under the brain scrambling influence of Morgan's skillful kisses and my escalating hormones if the applause hadn't broken into my concentration.

Is it still considered applause if only one person is clapping?

"Well played, Ms. Logan." Kane's tongue returned to its normal anatomical position in *his* mouth before he slowly pressed a soft kiss to my lips. As I unwound my legs from his waist and slid down the front of him like an ungainly pole dancer, I felt Kane's hard length punching out the front of his jeans against my stomach. Clearly, Satan wasn't the only one giving me a standing ovation.

Hey, we were having a moment. Don't judge me.

I favored my Hellhound with a brilliant smile

before turning in his arms to face the Devil. "But there is still the matter of Buddy's future to discuss."

"What's to discuss?" I flicked a glance at Buddy who began shifting nervously from one foot to the other. "The contract expired, Cerberus broke the rules, and we're here to take him home. Seems pretty cut and dried to me." Satan stepped closer bringing us nearly nose to nose.

In case you were worried, I'm happy to report the sad lack of oral hygiene in these parts did not extend to the Leader of the Banned.

As he lowered his voice and his breath fanned my face, I caught the warm, spicy aroma of black licorice. I'm personally not a huge fan of black licorice, but it was a definite improvement over the Eau de Butt my admirer Fluffy had been rocking while humping my leg.

"Listen, I can't just let the kid loose on the mortal world without someone taking responsibility. Despite what you might think, I'll be happy to see the back of him. Every single one of my dancers is susceptible, and he's been screwing with my chorus line every night. It's exhausting. I choreograph the Can-Can, and in the middle of the show they start doing the Macarena. Something's got to be done with him, and he's already failed at nearly every role he's been placed in. Of course, we haven't tried a Retriever yet."

There was a speculative gleam in those burning red eyes as he kept his gaze fixed on me. Me? Train Buddy as a Retriever? Hell, I didn't even know what *I* was doing. I bit my lip and glanced at Morgan. He shrugged helpfully. Well, the sight of his broad, muscular shoulders helped, his complete lack of response did not.

Dropping my head, I planted my hands on my hips, and stared at the dusty toes of my kick ass boots while I wracked my brain for a solution. And then it hit me. Of course everything still depended on Buddy, and wasn't that a comforting thought?

"Hey, Buddy." I motioned him over. He didn't limp over quite as quickly this time and he gave the Midnight Idol a wide berth, carefully keeping Kane and me between him and Satan. "What would *you* like to do?"

"Huh?" He gaped with of the most impressive deer-in-the-headlights expressions I'd ever seen. Wucking fonderful.

"Well, you've apprenticed in a number of supernatural positions. Have any of them appealed to you? Was there any particular one you think maybe you'd want to pursue?" His lips compressed into a thin line, and he slowly shook his head from side to side. All righty then.

"Well, Mr. Newton suggests maybe I could train you as a Retriever. Would you like that?"

"No offense, Ms. Logan, but I really don't want to be a Retriever. Besides, I'm not all that sure you even know what *you're* doing."

Well, wasn't he a perceptive little shit?

Clearly he was wise beyond his years to realize the Retriever's Guide According to Max Logan was not his best bet. So what was left? He still had a psychosocial developmental stage to master, and I uneasily suspected that even after all we'd been through already, Satan was not going to release him easily unless we came up with a plan.

"Kane, a little help here?" I whispered out of the

side of my mouth.

"You're doing fine, Logan." While his easy trust gave me the warm fuzzies, I couldn't help thinking slightly less faith and a few helpful suggestions would not be unwelcome.

"Buddy, do you like being the Zombie King?" Kane asked, finally.

"I hate it," the kid mumbled miserably. "Do you think accidentally controlling the minds and actions of your classmates when you're mad or upset makes high school any easier? Do you think it impresses a girl when you take her parking at the cemetery and corpses pop up around the car offering to serve you? Well, it doesn't. It sucks."

"You took a girl parking at the cemetery?" Surpassing my surprise that he'd gotten a date in the first place was my conviction I had to find him a new make-out spot. I was definitely not up for playing Whack-A-Mole in the graveyard every time he got lucky.

"Focus, Ms. Logan."

Why did people keep saying that to me?

"Since you're the first ones who've ever even bothered to ask, I'll tell you. I don't want to be the Zombie King. And I may not have any idea yet what I do want to do, but I do know exactly what I want to *be*. I want to be normal. At least for a while, maybe until I'm old enough to figure it all out. Can you make that happen?"

"You can't change who and what you are, son," Morgan said, dropping a hand on Buddy's thin shoulder. "Not really."

"Well, if I can't then why does everyone keep

trying to make me?" the kid snapped bitterly, but his eyes glinted suspiciously as he looked up at the Grim Reaper.

"Because there's no one like you to teach you the ropes, and they're afraid of what you can do," I said thoughtfully. Just like me. I'd been so angry about being lied to, but in retrospect, my parents had done me an incredible favor. They'd loved me enough to give me normal. Buddy had spent a lifetime surrounded by people who were more concerned with their own interests than his. I rubbed my palm absently over my sternum to soothe the ache I felt there. Seventeen years of loveless loneliness learning that even negative attention was preferable to no attention. He deserved better. Didn't everyone? I pinched the bridge of my nose between my thumb and forefinger. All these freakin' emotional revelations and learning experiences were giving me a migraine.

"You're sure?" I took a deep breath. "You really would give up your powers?"

"In a heartbeat," he replied firmly, straightening his shoulders and appearing more certain and mature than I'd ever seen him. "I might still be a screwed up teenager, but at least I'd be the same as every other screwed up teenager, right?"

"Right, but that's generally a temporary malady and to the best of my knowledge has never caused a Zombie Apocalypse. At least I've never read about it. So how does it work?" My head swiveled back and forth between Satan and Morgan. Judging by the blank expressions on both their faces, they were not following my train of thought. Clearly it was one of those singular occasions when my brain actually functions in advance of my mouth.

What? It happens.

"Sorry?" Morgan's high smooth brow pleated in confusion.

"Binding his powers. How do we neutralize the Zombie King and take him off the supernatural radar so everyone leaves him alone until he's ready?" Satan opened his mouth and I rounded on him like a bear protecting her cub. "And don't even try to tell me it can't be done. I spent thirty-five years with no one the wiser, including me, so why can't Buddy?"

"Beautiful and brilliant, too. You really are the total package, Logan," Morgan laughed.

"Preaching to the choir, Reaper. You may reward me later at which time I might allow you a glimpse of my other hidden talents." I offered him a slow flirtatious wink before turning my attention back to the Lord of the Underworld. "So spill, Wayne. What's it going to take?"

"Well, first of all, both I and my, er counterpart..." He glanced upward nervously. "Both of us would have to approve it. Clearly, He would have no problem with it. I mean, let's be honest, a Zombie Apocalypse is more in keeping with my bucket list than His."

"Okay, so if His approval is a given, then there's no problem, right? Just wave your magic pitchfork or whatever it is you do and let's get on with it."

"His approval is a given, mine is not."

"Whatchoo talkin' bout, Beelzebub?"

"Oh, that's very good, Ms. Logan. Reaper, be sure to bring her down for Seventies Sitcom Week. She'll be awesome." Satan leaned in close, too close.

Can we spell personal space, boys and girls?

"Your uncanny ability to channel child stars aside, don't forget who you're talking to, young lady. Do you have even an ounce of self-preservation rattling around in that pretty head of yours?"

Satan thought my head was pretty, too? I was having a banner day. I momentarily wondered if I should ask what he thought of my ass and then decided if the low growl clawing its way out of Kane's chest was any indication, I should probably put a cork in my curiosity. But I digress. And yes, I had an ounce of self-preservation, in fact, most days I had at least a good two liter bottle of it sloshing around somewhere, but this wasn't about saving me, this was about saving Buddy. Satan's too close face began to morph and waver. Suddenly he didn't resemble Wayne Newton at all. Well, shit! Turns out Satan really *is* scary enough to curl a bald man's hair. Who knew? Sister Myrtle Elephant would be so relieved. I took a quick step back and crashed into Morgan's chest.

"Knock it off, Luc. You know you won't touch her because it will piss me off, and that in turn, is sure to make Celina very unhappy. I think we can all agree that is never pretty," Morgan growled.

"Well, well, well, another country heard from. I wondered how long you were going to stand there like an impotent prick and let your woman do all the thinking."

"You know exactly how much of a prick I can be, and I've got nothing to prove to you or anyone here. On any level. Logan doesn't need me to speak for her and she knows I've got her back. So how about you knock off the Hey-look-at-me-I'm-the-big-scary-Devil crap and get to the point."

"I just want to be sure Ms. Logan understands that Wayne Newton, like everything else here is thinly-contrived artifice. In general, Hell is not a fun place, and I am not a warm and fuzzy guy." He straightened away from me, and in the blink of an eye, the full-blown illusion was back.

I sure wished I could do that. I'd be looking like the tall, cool blonde in that French perfume commercial all day long.

"Correction. I *am* warm. Actually, I'm downright hot. But fuzzy? Yeah, not so much. But Kane does have a point. My underworld is a much nicer place when his mother is a happy camper. I do see the logic in binding the kid, and I may even agree it's the best solution, but I have an image to uphold, you dig? My cooperation requires a sacrifice."

"Of course it does," I muttered. What in the name of black cherry ice cream made me think anything about this whole fiasco would be simple? Of course, maybe he'd want a pound of flesh. Considering I was fully committed to initiating wild monkey sex with the Grim Reaper after we got home, maybe I could persuade him to take an extra ten? "What do you want?"

"Well." Satan stroked Wayne Newton's chin and narrowed his eyes. "I strongly suspect my Guardian will be out of commission for a while by the time my darling wife is through with him. I'm going to need a temp, and the employment agencies down here are so unreliable. I need someone with a bit of experience. Morgan, you should do nicely."

"Fine," Kane said tersely.

"No way. I won't leave you here," I babbled at the

same time, my eyes widening in horror as I spun to face Morgan. My words didn't come out nearly as forcefully as planned. Hyperventilation has that effect on me.

Kane buried his hands in my hair, soothing his thumbs along my jaw, and touching his forehead to mine. The look in his eyes bore no resemblance to the panicked expression I knew I must be sporting. If anything, he looked slightly amused.

"Baby, it's fine. I was born here, remember? Couple of days, a week tops, and I'll be home. Celina won't kill Harvey, she'll just make him wish for death. He'll shift, he'll heal, and the debt will be paid. Right, Luc?"

"Sure. Probably."

Kane stared into my eyes as though he could communicate his reassurance directly into my heart. I wanted to believe him, I did, but this was Hell, and Satan himself had just informed me nothing was as it seemed. I curled my fingers into the front of his shirt and drew him even closer, wanting to crawl right inside and stay there. I'd found someone to give my heart to, someone who actually got me, only to have him taken away. Again. It wasn't fair. I hadn't been able to save Roger, but this wasn't death. This was politics. And when politics are involved, there's always potential for a filibuster. This time I was fighting for what was mine.

Chapter 20

"Are you a gambling man, Wayne?" I laid my hand on Morgan's cheek for just a moment before pulling away and spinning back to face the Devil. I might not win, but I had to try.

"I've been known to toss the dice on occasion," Satan shrugged with a grin. "Are you proposing a wager, Ms. Logan?"

"Um, yes. Yes, I am." Dice? Well, I didn't know anything about dice, but I did know something about cards. And if I was wrong? My odds were still fifty-fifty at worst. It was certainly better than nothing.

"Logan, what do you think you're doing?" Morgan's tone sounded amused, and his big hands dropped onto my shoulders and began a slow, rhythmic stroking as he turned me back to face him. Frankly, all this rotating back and forth between the Grim Reaper and the Prince of Darkness was making me dizzy. "Take Buddy, go home, and get him settled. That alone should keep you busy for a while. There's more room at my place, so grab your cat and wait for me there if you want. Really, this is not a big deal."

Moisture pricked the back of my lids. Leaving the man I loved in the afterlife felt painfully familiar, and no amount of reassurance could completely assuage the fear.

Yeah, I know you thought I was a tough mofo, but

you were probably fooled by that big box of crazy I carry around. And the leather.

I sucked in a deep, shaky breath and commenced rapid blinking.

Have I mentioned I don't do tears?

Not in public, and most definitely not in front of Wayne Newton and the Sin City South chorus line. I felt something warm and wet trickle down my cheek and resigned myself to my impending mortification. Perhaps I'd given myself too much credit.

Tell me this surprises you.

Apparently, I did do tears. In public *and* in front of Wayne Newton and the Sin City South chorus line. I hate when that happens.

"Yes, it is a big deal, dammit! I'm hot and hungry. And not in a good way. You can't just wave a piece of chocolate lava cake with hot fudge sauce and whipped cream under a girl's nose and then refuse to give her a fork. It's cruel and inhumane. I'm an instant gratification kind of girl. Besides, this is Satan we're talking about. Is there anyone more likely to strategically redirect the truth?"

"Do you trust me, Logan?"

"Of course I trust *you*. It's Wayne Newton I have a tiny problem with. How do I know his ass isn't just sucking buttermilk?"

"Go home," he laughed, thumbing a tear from my cheek. "I know what this is about, but I'm not dead, just temporarily detained. I *will* come back to you. And I promise you can have all the chocolate lava cake with hot fudge sauce and whipped cream you want. I'll bring you the whole damn fork drawer. Deal?"

"Real whipped cream? Not that fake non-dairy

product that can double as modeling clay when it sits too long?" I sniffed, wrapping my arms around his waist and burying my face in his chest. "'Cause that doesn't, you know, work for me at all."

"With sprinkles," he promised solemnly. Sprinkles? Saints preserve us, the man truly was my other half. I knuckled the moisture from my eyes and tried to smile.

"Are you sure you don't want me to win you in a game of cards? I mean, I've had a lot of time on my hands over the last year and the Internet is my friend. Sure, some card designs are harder to read than others, but none are cheat proof, and I've memorized every configuration there is. I can do this, Morgan. This is Hell, after all. What do you think the chances are the gambling is on the up and up?"

"Slim to none. And while I'm equally impressed and appalled by your unexpected grasp of the illegal and underhanded, no matter how good you are, you can't win. Trying to beat the Devil at his own game is an exercise in futility. Now, take Buddy and get on the boat. Go back the way we came and hang a left at the clearing. There's a small pond there you can use as a portal."

"But what if Cerberus…" I was stalling, and we both knew it. Still, he seemed to understand my desperate need for reassurance whether or not he considered it reasonable.

"Thanks to your clever strategy, my cousin is now in the doghouse, both literally and figuratively. The only reason I let him get the upper hand the last time was because I didn't know where he'd stashed my sister. You really need to have some faith in my abilities, Logan. Anyway, don't worry about him. You put him right in the crosshairs of my mother's cray-dar, and I suspect he'll be keeping a very low profile for a while."

I gazed deeply into those amazing emerald eyes, searching for even the slightest bit of subterfuge or uncertainty. I didn't find any. Maybe he was right and this was just a speed bump in the road to our happily-ever-after. Maybe it wasn't a big deal, and by the time I got Buddy situated, everything would be back to normal, at least our version of it, and he would be home.

Yeah, that crap again.

I decided to pull up my big girl panties—mostly because I didn't have much of a choice—and believe him. I pulled them up figuratively of course, because I wasn't wearing any, since the ass-tastick fit of my leather pants required me to go full commando in order to avoid VPL's.

That's Visible Panty Lines for those of you unacquainted with the peculiar afterlife affinity for acronyms. You're welcome.

"Okay."

"Okay?"

"Yeah, okay," I sighed. "I'll take Buddy, get on the boat, find the clearing, whip out the fugly necklace, and jump in the pond. I'll set up camp at your place, re-enroll the kid in school, and find him a tutor so he can catch up in time to graduate. Hell, I'll even talk to Bob Grubly about taking him back part-time at the Supersave. Happy?"

"Yeah, I am," he smiled. "I love you, Logan. You're going to make a great mother someday."

And there it was. The big honking arrow floating just outside my happy waiting to burst my bubble. I would never be a mother, great or otherwise. I gasped as my heart, which had been so filled with possibility just moments ago, suddenly shriveled into a hard, painful lump. The truth smacked me in the head moments later, and it hurt almost as much. I wretched my gaze away from Kane's, looking around wildly until I located Wayne Newton.

"You said every binding requires a sacrifice. That's what they gave up, isn't it? My parents. The price of my binding was my fertility."

The answer was there in Wayne Newton's intense red eyes without him uttering a single word. It made perfect sense, of course. They'd had to bind my powers. How could my father, a human, have any hope of raising a supernatural child alone? And since I'd been clueless, how would I? But understanding the reasoning didn't prevent the disappointment of every negative test, every failed treatment, and every little pee stick that had never turned blue from rushing back. It didn't undo being poked, prodded, and progesteroned to death only to discover I was the defective one, I was the piece of the pregnancy puzzle that didn't fit. How easy it had been to concentrate on my superhero superpowers and fabulous attire and conveniently forget the simple truth that I was flawed, I was broken. I'd always believed Roger deserved better. And Morgan did, too.

"Listen," I turned back to Morgan but kept my eyes plastered to his shirtfront. No way did I want to deal with the disappointed expression I knew he must be wearing. "I should have told you. I mean, I wasn't trying to hide it, exactly. I...well, it just never came up in conversation, you know? But now you know…well, I get that you didn't realize what you were signing on for. Really, it's fine. I'll just take Buddy to my place. It's closer to the Supersave anyway, and it's in his old school district and…"

"Don't."

I hadn't expected him to react with sunshine and rainbows, but the harsh anger in his voice took me by surprise. One arm hooked around my waist while the other hand gripped my chin painfully and forced my head back until I had no choice but to meet his eyes. They positively glowed, and not in a good way. His sculpted jaw was clenched tightly enough to crush bone, and his lips twisted in a teeth-baring snarl. Were those fangs?

Well shit! Clearly, he was going to make a fine temporary Guardian of the Gates of Hell. Morgan Kane in full-on-pissed-mode was pretty freakin' scary. Who knew?

"Don't you dare crawl inside yourself over this again and shut me out. The last time you did, it cost you your marriage and almost destroyed your soul in the bargain. I know it hurts. I know it's important to you, and it totally sucks. I would fix it for you if I could, but do not presume to tell me how I feel about it. I fell in love with *you*, Logan. I didn't fall in love with your damn uterus. So don't even think about taking up self-sabotage as a hobby again, is that clear?"

It would have been a heck of a lot clearer if I didn't have the big black spots swimming in front of my eyes. Apparently, Morgan felt very strongly I should not allow my insecurities related to my inability to procreate to impact our relationship. Perhaps a bit too strongly. Even skirting the edges of consciousness, I knew he would never intentionally hurt me, but at the moment, he was six and a half feet of Hellhound in danger of squeezing the life out of my measly, just over five feet, until I concurred. Which I might have contemplated doing if I was capable of speech.

"Can't breathe," I croaked and felt the welcome relief of air rushing into my starving lungs as he immediately loosened his hold. I sagged against him, sucking in oxygen and waiting for it to replenish my brain cells while I mulled over what he'd said. He refused to allow me to take up self-sabotage as a hobby again. *Again.*

"How long have you known?" I hauled back and socked him in the gut. Yes, his stomach was as solid as steel. Yes, I'd forgotten to keep my thumb out. Yes, it hurt me far worse than it hurt him. At least I assumed it did since I winced and shook out my hand while he didn't as much as flinch. Bad doggie.

"Since you filled in for Alicia as the Superintendent of Spiritual Impediment. I had to approve the temporary appointment, and it was in your file. Despite appearances at the Office of Central Processing, the afterlife records are actually quite accurate and well organized. Is your hand okay?"

"Define okay. Why didn't you ever say anything?"

"Like you said, it never came up. What exactly would you have had me say? Hi Logan, nice dress, how's your barren womb?" He quirked a brow.

"I suppose that might have been a little awkward," I agreed with a small smile, wrapping my arms around his waist and resting my cheek over his heart. "So if you already knew, why did you say I'd be a great mother someday?"

"Because I believe it. The qualities required for motherhood aren't dependent on a functional set of anatomical parts, Logan. You're the self-proclaimed Internet queen. Haven't you ever seen the viral video of the cat nursing the ducklings?"

"Ducklings cannot suckle," I snorted.

Seriously, did he spend so much time severing souls that he never got a chance to watch cable?

"Of course they can't. That's my point. Motherhood isn't dependent upon the birth canal. The behavior comes from the heart regardless of the species or the biology involved."

"Roger said something like that once. He said people don't have to share DNA to be a family," I sighed. "It really doesn't matter to you, does it?"

He'd known before he ever met me. He'd had the choice, and he was still here. That should count for something, right? Maybe it was time to stop hating myself for everything I'm not and concentrate on being the best of what I am.

"Roger was a smart guy. And no, it doesn't. The only thing about it that bothers me is knowing how much it hurts you."

"Yeah it does, but maybe not quite as much as it used to." I stretched up on my toes and pressed my lips to his chin. It was the best I could do from my limited height without further accommodation on his part.

"Well, this is all just too tender and romantic for words, but I have an unguarded gate, and Charon's been holding the boat for ten minutes. Let's move it along shall we, boys and girls?" Satan clapped his hands together, and the small crowd scattered, presumably to prepare for the upcoming show. Having been privy to a taste of Lucifer's vocal stylings on my arrival, I couldn't say I'd be sorry to miss it.

"A week, right? No longer."

I reached up for a handful of Morgan's silky hair and tugged his lips down to mine. His hand slid around to the nape of my neck, and he deepened the kiss. His tongue traced the seam of my lips and then swept inside, seeking, stroking, plundering, as if he couldn't get enough of me. I released his hair and raised a hand to his unshaven cheek, the stubble rasped against my fingertips, and his breath stuttered at my touch. He pulled me closer, hitching me up by the waist before tearing his mouth away with a pained groan while his heart hammered frantically against my palm. His breathing was as harsh and ragged as mine, and when he sighed, it sounded more like a growl vibrating in his chest.

"A week," he agreed hoarsely shifting his attention to the pier to where Buddy, clearly not willing to run the risk of being left behind, was already clambering aboard the boat. With every ounce of strength I possessed, I turned away and followed him up the ramp. Hanging over the rail, I dug in my pocket and tossed Kane what remained of my bag of chocolate covered beans. He caught them easily, and a grin split his face.

"You might get hungry," I called as we chugged away.

"I don't think they're going to cut it," he called back with a wink.

"Remember, Kane...a week. This better not turn out to be a strategic redirection of the truth, or no chocolate lava cake with hot fudge sauce and whipped cream for you."

He threw his head back, and I think he laughed, but it was hard to tell. First of all because the oddly accelerated rate of speed at which we were traveling had already reduced Morgan and Wayne to two tiny specks on the shore, and secondly because the copious tears I was absolutely not crying in public were all but blinding me.

Thankfully, I still gripped the rail as the boat bumped against the dock on the opposite shore, knocking me off-balance. Buddy, who'd remained beside me, yet sympathetically silent during my two point seven minute meltdown on the trip across the water, now reached for my hand and I took it with an appreciative, if watery, smile. I'm only human. All things considered, I suppose it was okay to have a meltdown as long as I didn't unpack it and try to live there. Again. At least it wouldn't take long to disembark. We were the only two passengers on board for the return trip. I guess Hell was the afterlife version of a roach motel. You checked in, but you didn't check out. No surprise there. What *was* a surprise was the gorgeous pirate rocking braids, a red bandana, and a leather tricorn hat who stepped forward with sharply sculpted cheekbones and a flirtatious wink to lower the gangplank.

"At yer service, love."

Chapter 21

Almost two weeks later, after gently persuading Buddy to let us take him to a dermatologist, a competent orthodontist, and a good hair stylist, he was a different kid.

Okay, so maybe it was Gail's gentle persuasion, and my suggesting that it was time to stop rocking the dork, but Buddy and I understand one another and whatever works, you know?

Besides, going shopping with Denise and trying the new contact lenses had been his idea. Needless to say, allowing Denise to get involved pretty much guaranteed the reclamation of Buddy Jenks was an expensive proposition. But I had all that money just sitting in the bank gathering interest anyway. Though I still wasn't entirely comfortable spending it indiscriminately on myself, I discovered it didn't bother me at all when Buddy was the beneficiary.

He'd decided to enroll in the high school nearer Kane's place where we were staying. I think he wanted a fresh start, and I couldn't honestly say I blamed him. Surprisingly, Buddy is an incredibly bright peg as long as he's not being forced into an ill-fitting hole. But the biggest change in Buddy had nothing to do with his appearance, the biggest change was in the kid, himself. With a family and a home, he belonged in a way he never had before, a way most of us take for granted. For perhaps the first time in his life, he was actually happy—well and truly happy. It was a beautiful thing.

"I'm home." The front door slammed me out of my reverie. I took a sip of coffee that didn't approach the perfection of the Grim Reaper's, and turned away from my contemplation of the gathering dusk beyond the kitchen window.

"In here," I called, seconds before Buddy skidded into the kitchen, tossing his hoodie over the back of one of the mismatched chairs, and his books on the farmhouse table.

"Isn't Dad coming in? How was work?"

"Nah, he said to tell you he'll see you Sunday. He's going to teach me how to use power tools."

Oh, swell. I made a mental note to send in that health insurance application. Buddy flashed me a toothy grin, revealing the clear plastic braces that had replaced the purple monstrosities, and he scooted around me to grab a cola from the fridge. I shook my head at the sight of the baggy blue jeans hanging off his skinny butt below the hem of his plain black tee. Propping a hip against the counter across from me, he took a long swig. Denise had assured me that's the way the kids wear them now. Who was I to question the Fashion Maven?

"Try not to cut off anything you might have a future use for, m'kay?"

While Bob Grubly had generously offered Buddy his old job at the Supersave, the former Zombie King had instantly bonded with the current Hardware King, and he'd jumped at a part-time position at Logan's Hardware, instead. My father informed me he could use the help since I'd inconsiderately taken a sabbatical of indeterminate length on my return from Hell. But, I think the more likely reason was that after so many years of being the only testosterone producing member of our family, Dad was secretly delighted to have a boy in the mix.

"Sure. Oh, by the way, Mr. Grubly stopped in today. He said to remind you his wife still works over at the Curl Up and Dye, and they're running a special on color this week. There's a coupon in the paper."

"Yeah, so?"

"Well." He raised his bottle to his lips to hide the smirk. "He said he couldn't help noticing a few gray hairs when you came by to talk to him about my job."

"Is that right? Well, the next time you see Bob Grubly you tell him I said thanks, but no thanks. I simply believe in early holiday preparation, and I'm growing my own tinsel. Got it?"

Soda spewed from Buddy's nose. I yanked a handful of paper towels from the stainless steel holder and handed them over wordlessly. After wiping his face and mopping the floor, he crumpled the towels and shot a perfect three pointer into the trash.

"Sure thing. So let's see, today's forecast is mouthy and sarcastic with a chance of rudeness. Obviously there's been no word from Morgan," he observed, while screwing the top on the bottle and putting it back in the fridge.

I shook my head and turned away to rinse my coffee cup in the sink, then gripped the edge of the counter and dropped my chin to my chest. No, there'd been no word, and it was well into the second week. Every day I woke up in the morning, straightened the house, though it didn't need it, and watched daytime

TV until my brain turned to mush. After that, with nothing left to occupy me, I would creep into Morgan's office and stare at the mirror as though I could will him to walk through it. And every day I saw nothing but a clear, crisp reflection of my own pale face and shadowed eyes in the glass.

The first week hadn't been so bad, but once the unofficial deadline had passed, the squirrels in my head started running wild, stirring up all of the old insecurities in a fight for my attention. I tossed them a handful of nuts and told them to back off. Morgan said he'd return, and he would. But while I absolutely believed it, I still hadn't managed to pencil patience in to my list of virtues. Last night, after finding me asleep on the floor in front of the mirror for the third time in as many days, Buddy insisted on dragging the damn thing into the bedroom. Well, at least I'd be comfortable.

I'd even considered heading over to visit the Timekeeper for gin and cookies just in case she'd heard anything. But let's face it that was just one step away from skipping the cookies altogether and finding some half-baked excuse to take another slide down the Drop of Doom. And didn't that just smack of desperation? I refused to be that girl anymore.

"You know what they say about a watched pot? I'm pretty sure it applies to mirrors, too. So why don't we watch a movie or something instead?" He suggested.

"Sure. You pick the movie. I'll make the popcorn." I pasted a smile on my face as I turned around and skated my sock clad feet across the tile to the pantry cabinet. He grinned back happily, waggled his brows, and headed for the den. The sound of the cabinet door opening apparently alerted Sir Chicken Caesar to the possibility of food. He hauled himself to his feet and waddled over from the fireplace, and he then attempted the first loop of an ungainly figure eight around my ankles just as I was turning back to the microwave. With a nifty series of dance maneuvers, and a spot on imitation of a ceiling fan, I managed to avoid serious injury, but my obese feline remained unimpressed and simply plopped his butt on the floor and yawned. I'd worried a change of environment at his advanced age would be traumatic, but he hadn't batted an eye. In fact, I'm not sure he bothered to open an eye. As long as there's sufficient food and available staff, I guess he's flexible. I tossed the popcorn in the microwave, sprinkled a couple of kitty treats in Caesar's blue pottery bowl, and scratched him between the ears. He, of course, offered me a bland stare, hissed, and proceeded to chow down his goodies.

"Nothing too gory," I called out over the hum of the microwave while the scent of freshly popped corn filled the kitchen. "And no horror films, because we're, you know, out here in the middle of the nowhere, and I won't sleep a wink. Oh, and definitely nothing complicated requiring my undivided attention. And no romances. Definitely no romances."

"Maybe a nice documentary about watching paint dry?" Buddy's voice drifted into the kitchen.

Frankly, I was a little worried I was starting to rub off on him.

"What color paint?"

"So we'll be watching the same thing. Again. Is it still in the DVD player?" He reappeared in the doorway and headed for the hallway leading to the bedrooms.

"I'm going to get changed first."

"Hey, it's a classic," I said to his retreating back. There was no reason for me to change. I was already wearing an oversized T-shirt and a pair of flannel boxer shorts along with my fuzzy red socks. I'd given serious consideration to getting dressed after my shower this morning, but it had just seemed like a wasted effort and now it was paying off. Clearly a stroke of accidental genius on my part. Fortunately, I hadn't been called upon to leave the house. Wearing boxer shorts and red fuzzy socks in public with any kind of dignity is impossible.

By the time I'd managed to tear open the popcorn bag, run cold water on the steam burns I acquired while doing so, and juggle the bowl and two bottles of water into the bedroom, Buddy had already changed into a T-shirt and a pair of sweats. He'd also set up the DVD player and propped himself against the headboard on one side of the king-sized bed with the remote at the ready. I set a bottle of water on the oak night table on my side of the bed, tossed the other to him, and then plopped the bowl between us before climbing up on my own side.

I settled back against the enormous mound of pillows as Buddy hit the play button and the music began. I realize not everyone can chair dance while lying in bed, but I was just awesome like that.

Tell me this surprises you.

"Really? Again?" He frowned, grabbing the popcorn bowl and wrapping his arms around it protectively when my gyrations threatened to flip it upside down. I appreciated his quick thinking since I was still discovering the un-popped kernels from my previous dance recitals. Usually under my left hip at around three in the morning, right after I actually had managed to fall asleep.

Yeah, that.

"Clearly you have no musicality whatsoever. It's a well-established fact it's physically impossible to sit still during any rendition of this theme song."

"Clearly you are stuck in the eighties. So, I asked a girl to prom today." He slipped it in oh-so-casually, but there was a warm flush creeping up his neck and a shy smile hovering around his lips as he glanced at me from the corner of his eyes. "She, uh…she said yes."

"Oh, Buddy! That's so great!" Instinctively I reached to hug him, but ended up patting him on the arm instead. "So what color is her dress? We'll have to order flowers. What kind does she want? And what about the tickets? Do you think we should rent a limo, or do you think that's too over the top…?"

"Max! Sheesh! Slow down. I've got this. You've already spent a fortune on me. Not that I don't appreciate it, but I'm working now and I'll take care of it," he laughed.

"Well, maybe we could split the cost then?" I insisted. "I mean, I can't take it with me, right? Well, I guess I can, but we've both seen where that gets a person."

"Stop." He shook his head with a smile and reached for my hand. "You've already given me everything. I have a home. I have people who care what happens to me, and a life to call my own. It's the only thing I ever wanted, something I gave up hoping for, a long time ago. You had less reason than anyone to stick your neck out for me, and yet you did. And not because there was anything in it for you. You've given me normal, Max. I can spend the rest of my life trying, but I can't ever repay that. So thank you. Well, thank you doesn't seem to cut it, but I just wanted you to know."

"Well, shit!"

That's me, spouting profundity at every opportunity.

Honestly, I was at a loss for words.

Yes, we have already established that in itself is a rare event.

No matter what tomorrow might bring, no matter how many mistakes I'd yet to make, I would always be able to look back on this moment and remember I'd managed to do one thing completely right. In spite of myself. I squeezed Buddy's thin fingers across the top of the plaid flannel comforter and stared straight ahead with my throat aching, blinking rapidly as a banana was shoved in an unmarked police car's tailpipe.

This movie is genius. Seriously.

The little snot leaned forward and regarded me with suspicion. "Are you crying?"

"Of course not," I sniffed, turning my face away. Clearly, my heart simply was so full it was leaking from my eyes. "I don't do tears. At least not in public and certainly not in front of a smart ass former Zombie King."

"Uh, huh. I suppose you don't do sarcasm either?" I heard the smile in his voice.

"Absolutely not. I'm simply a highly skilled professional who excels at pointing out the obvious to the oblivious. It's a gift."

"Lucky me."

"Indeed." I sniffed, knowing when all was said and

done, I was the lucky one. "You're welcome. And Buddy? Thank you, too."

Epilogue

Saturday night, I found myself alone and abandoned. More so than usual anyway. Buddy had finagled a date with Prom Girl. Unbelievably, the Hardware King offered to loan him his classic muscle car. Yes, the one neither Denise nor I are allowed to touch. I tried not to be insulted. I guess I was never very good at being the son Dad always wanted. Buddy seemed to be doing a much better job. Because Dad insisted the vehicle would only be comfortable in its very own garage stall, the kid was camping at their place tonight, and I planned to head over tomorrow and bring him back after the Logan family Sunday morning post-church coffee klatch.

I was surprised to discover I actually missed the kid's company. I lasted about twenty minutes into the movie before deciding that though I loved the comedic genius of it with the intensity of a thousand suns, reading the phone book was more stimulating at this point than the eighth screening of the same movie in as many days.

I clicked off the DVD with a sigh, tuned the television to the home improvement channel, and turned off the bedside lamp. I snuggled down in the vast emptiness of Kane's king-sized bed, and prepared to be enlightened. I'd renewed my friendship with the Internet and discovered recent reviews of functional magnetic resonance-imaging studies indicate subliminal stimuli activate specific regions of the brain despite the participant being unaware. Translation: I planned to learn the secret to successful gardening while I slept. Morgan would be so surprised. Of course, studies also suggest subliminal messages are more effective if they're goal-related and my actual interest in gardening was nonexistent. My awesome plan became irrelevant when I realized they were running a renovation marathon. Power tools and I have never been friends.

I pointed the remote at the television and clicked it off. The room was plunged into darkness. Well, except for the moonlight glinting off the solid silver surface of the mirror, aka the portal to the afterlife, mocking me from the corner of the room. Loving people and then being forced to miss them was exhausting. I'm no different from anyone else, seeking that one person who makes me feel important, who makes me feel I matter and am loved in a way no one else could possibly be. Love isn't just about finding someone you can live with, it's about finding someone you can't live without. It's about finding someone who makes you better without trying to change who you are. I'd been incredibly lucky to find it not once, but twice. All things considered, I suppose I have a lot of nerve whining about a couple of lonely nights.

I must have dozed off because I was startled awake by a cool draft as the comforter was lifted away and its warmth was replaced by two hard, sinewy arms snaking around my waist and a large, heated body enveloping mine from behind. Ordinarily, I would have been alarmed, but I'd been having this same dream for two weeks and if this was a repeat performance, I was in no hurry to wake up. Of course, the very real aroma of jelly doughnuts was a dead giveaway. The Grim Reaper was home at last.

"What do you think you're doing?" I murmured sleepily, as he buried his face in the side of my neck, sending a warm spiral of heat right to my toes.

"I think it's called spooning." Kane smiled against my skin.

"Spooning. I see. Well, you do realize spooning very often leads to forking? I hope you've come prepared with the appropriate condiments and utensils."

"Sweetheart, I've been thinking of nothing but chocolate lava cake with hot fudge sauce and whipped cream for almost two weeks. I'm packing a full set of cutlery."

He eased his big, Grim Reaper-ish form over mine, and I sank further into the mattress under his delicious weight with a soft sigh, wiggling happily against the firm ridge of flesh jutting against the fly of his jeans. He'd cleverly removed his shirt ahead of time, and I was finally rewarded with those miles and miles of smooth, golden shoulders under my eager hands. I stroked my palms over his chest and—*Why hello, abs!* Grazing his impressive washboard with a light, teasing touch, I continued my exploration until my fingers tangled in the coarse line of crisp, curling hair disappearing into the waistband of his jeans.

His eyes locked on mine, and a wicked smile curved his lips. "Are you finished yet?"

"Not even close, why?" I grinned back.

"Because I'm waiting for my turn, and my patience has about reached its limit." He growled, grasping the hem of my T-shirt and yanking it over my head in one smooth motion. I arched against him in breathless delight, pressing the aching part of me to the aching part of him. My girlie bits nearly exploded with joy as he pressed back and lowered his lips to mine.

People say love hurts. Someone even wrote a song about it.

You're probably thinking of the 1975 hit, but the song was actually recorded long before that in 1960, and covered again in 1961.

But I digress. People are wrong. Rejection hurts. Loneliness hurts. Loss hurts. I guess they get confused. It isn't the love that hurts, it's the absence of it. In the end, love is the one thing that makes all those other hurts disappear.

"What took you so long?" I gasped as my boxers quickly met the same fate as my T-shirt. Kane paused in the act of tossing his jeans over the side of the bed.

"Celina's enthusiasm exceeded everyone's expectations. Harvey's still out of commission, but knowing how your mind works, I could almost hear the hamsters bouncing off the inside of your skull."

"They're squirrels," I giggled, tugging at the jeans. "And they're much tamer than they used to be."

"A rodent's a rodent." He grinned back. "Anyway, I insisted a certain leather-wearing, motorcycle riding high school dropout who defined cool find me a replacement."

"Seventies Sitcom Week?" I guessed. "And Celina is—wait, don't tell me—"

"Well, pink *is* her color." Morgan interrupted with a laugh and sent his pants sailing across the room. "How's the kid?"

"He's good. Really, really good. He'll be glad

you're back. I think he's had his fill of movie re-runs. He and Dad have totally hit it off. In fact, right at this moment…"

"At this moment—" Morgan interrupted, settling himself between my thighs and pinning my hands above my head while feathering a slow trail of kisses along my collarbone. He really was quite adept at multitasking. "I think we should concentrate on less talk-y, more cake-y."

I tried to respond with an enthusiastic *Hell, yeah,* but words were already beyond me. Tomorrow would come, and there would be problems to solve, mountains to climb, and dragons to slay, but for tonight, I let complete contentment have its way with me. Life is a cycle, and sometimes there's no easy—only different degrees of hard. But sometimes there's perfect, and I was ready to get me some. Not every couple can say they've been to Hell and back, together…and mean it. Literally. But we could. Sometimes the road you travel doesn't lead to the destination you expected. Lord knows, my road's been riddled with more twists than a five-pound tray of pasta salad. But if you can look back on the trip and still smile at the end…then maybe it was worth it. As I melted into the arms of my Grim Reaper, and his lips settled on mine, believe me, I was smiling.

A word about the author...

Sharon Saracino was born and raised in the beautiful anthracite coal region of Northeastern Pennsylvania. A lifelong love of writing took a back seat to real life while she got married, raised a family, went back to college, and finally decided what she wanted to be when she grew up! The oldest of three siblings, she was raised in a small town rich in history and filled with characters galore.

Sharon is a member of Pennwriters, Romance Writers of America, the Fantasy, Futuristic, and Paranormal Chapter, and the Maryland Romance Writers.

When she is not reading, writing, or dabbling in photography and genealogy, she works full time as a Certified Registered Rehabilitation Nurse. She plans to win the lottery just as soon as she remembers to buy a ticket, fantasizes about moving to Italy, brews limoncello, and spends time with her incredible husband, funny and talented son, and two crazy dogs.

http://sharonsaracino.com